The
Angel
Next Door
Spoils Me
Rotten

Saekisan
ILLUSTRATION BY
Hanekoto

Contents

The Path We've Walked Thus Far	001
Someone Similar but Different	015
Rome Wasn't Built in a Day	037
Fleeting Dreams and Cruelties of Youth	049
Cute Kids	063
Unwanted Contact	083
The More You Polish It, the More It Shines	095
From the Outside, They Seem…	111
Say the Name You'll Call Me Someday	137
A Secret Just for Two	155
Someone Who Looks Carefully	185
The Future We're Walking Into	207

Amane Fujimiya

A student who began living alone when he started high school. He's poor at every type of housework and lives a slovenly life. Has a low opinion of himself and tends to put himself down, but is kind at heart.

Mahiru Shiina

A classmate who lives in the apartment next door to Amane. The most beautiful girl in school; everyone calls her an "angel." Started cooking for Amane because she couldn't overlook his unhealthy lifestyle.

©Hanekoto

The Angel Next Door Spoils Me Rotten

8.5

Saekisan

ILLUSTRATION BY
Hanekoto

YEN ON
NEW YORK

The Angel Next Door Spoils Me Rotten 8.5

Saekisan

TRANSLATION BY NICOLE WILDER ✳ COVER ART BY HANEKOTO

This book is a work of fiction. Names, characters, places, and incidents are the product of the author's imagination or are used fictitiously. Any resemblance to actual events, locales, or persons, living or dead, is coincidental.

OTONARI NO TENSHISAMA NI ITSUNOMANIKA DAMENINGEN NI SARETEITA KEN Vol. 8.5
Copyright © 2023 Saekisan
Illustration © 2023 Hanekoto
All rights reserved.
Original Japanese edition published in 2023 by SB Creative Corp.
This English edition is published by arrangement with SB Creative Corp., Tokyo in care of Tuttle-Mori Agency, Inc., Tokyo.

English translation © 2025 by Yen Press, LLC

Yen Press, LLC supports the right to free expression and the value of copyright. The purpose of copyright is to encourage writers and artists to produce the creative works that enrich our culture.

The scanning, uploading, and distribution of this book without permission is a theft of the author's intellectual property. If you would like permission to use material from the book (other than for review purposes), please contact the publisher. Thank you for your support of the author's rights.

Yen On
150 West 30th Street, 6th Floor
New York, NY 10001

Visit us at yenpress.com ✳ facebook.com/yenpress ✳ twitter.com/yenpress
yenpress.tumblr.com ✳ instagram.com/yenpress

First Yen On Edition: May 2025
Edited by Yen On Editorial: Ivan Liang
Designed by Yen Press Design: Liz Parlett

Yen On is an imprint of Yen Press, LLC.
The Yen On name and logo are trademarks of Yen Press, LLC.

The publisher is not responsible for websites (or their content) that are not owned by the publisher.

Library of Congress Cataloging-in-Publication Data
Names: Saekisan, author. | Hanekoto, illustrator. | Wilder, Nicole, translator.
Title: The angel next door spoils me rotten / Saekisan ; illustration by Hanekoto ; translation by Nicole Wilder.
Other titles: Otonari no tenshi-sama ni Itsu no ma ni ka dame ningen ni sareteita ken. English
Description: First Yen On edition. | New York : Yen On, 2020– |
Identifiers: LCCN 2020043583 | ISBN 9781975319526 (v. 1 ; trade paperback) |
Subjects: CYAC: Love—Fiction.
Classification: LCC PZ7.1.S2413 An 2020 | DDC [Fic]—dc23
LC record available at https://lccn.loc.gov/2020043583

ISBNs: 979-8-8554-0886-7 (paperback)
979-8-8554-0887-4 (ebook)

10 9 8 7 6 5 4 3 2 1

LSC-C

Printed in the United States of America

The Path We've Walked Thus Far

Mahiru's pen brushed across the paper, making a scratching sound as she filled the blank white page with writing.

Beside her, Amane tried not to peek at what was being set down by the slim ballpoint pen grasped in Mahiru's dainty fingers as he watched her silently fill the thick book with words etched in black ink.

After they'd finished dinner and had cleaned up, the two of them were relaxing together. They weren't the type to be all over each other constantly. Their classmates, including the foolish Itsuki, had the wrong idea about them, and Amane wasn't sure whether to laugh about it or not. Apparently everyone thought Amane and Mahiru were getting frisky twenty-four hours a day.

The fact was, sometimes they did their own thing. They weren't always doing the same activity, or getting intimate. Even when they were sharing the same space, they spent a lot of peaceful time together pursuing their own interests.

That day was no exception, and although she had secured a seat by Amane's side, Mahiru was quietly absorbed in her writing.

Naturally, it would be rude of him to peek at her book, even if he was her boyfriend, so Amane wasn't trying to look, but he could tell she was writing something. Previously, she had written down the recipes for particular dishes and her thoughts on how the food turned out. But Mahiru wrote those in something else.

Glancing over, Amane could see this was a leather-bound book.

"What are you writing?"

He knew it was rude to interrupt her, but she had been focusing silently for quite a while, so without meaning to, he got curious and asked her about it. Mahiru immediately raised her head and gave him a strange look.

Then she saw Amane's gaze was lingering near her hands, and she made a small noise of understanding.

"Ah. This is my diary…I guess you could call it. I thought I'd better write down what happened today before I forget."

"Wow, that's so dedicated or, like, thoughtful of you."

It made perfect sense to Amane that it was her diary, and sure enough, once she mentioned it, Amane could see the book in her hands did look like one. It wasn't especially cute or pretty, like the kind many high school girls preferred. Instead, it looked dignified and sturdy, which he thought was very fitting for Mahiru.

She must have taken good care of it, because although it looked like she'd had the diary for quite a long time, it didn't show excessive wear. At least Amane didn't think it was something she had just picked up recently.

"Do you write in it every day?"

"No, not that frequently, only when something happens that's worth recording. I guess it's just a habit I've had since I was little…"

"I think it's great. If you make a note about what happened on a given day, then later when you think back on it, you'll know what went on."

"I write down the good and the bad, though."

Amane had never gone so far as to keep a diary, but whenever he wanted to make a memo about something, he jotted it down in the scheduling app on his smartphone. Doing so was helpful to him when he thought back on things later.

"I just think it's the perfect way to organize my feelings and information about my life. If I write it down here, I can quickly recall what happened, you see. I wrote an entry when we first met, Amane...or rather, the first time we ever talked."

"Let me guess—it was just one line... 'What the hell's wrong with this guy?'"

The first time he had ever spoken with Mahiru was the day he handed her his umbrella.

Thinking back on it now, he was sure he had been brusque and standoffish. He couldn't have made a particularly good impression, he thought. From Mahiru's perspective, it must have been certifiably awful.

To begin with, she didn't talk about it much, but on that day, Mahiru had been sitting alone in that park after a terrible confrontation with her mother. So it couldn't have felt very good to have someone come up and talk to her with that kind of bluntness, when she had just been hurt.

The more he thought back on it, the more he began to feel regret as he wondered why he couldn't have had a better attitude, but Mahiru looked at Amane's face and smiled. She seemed amused.

"Heh-heh, I won't deny it, but my impression of you wasn't that bad. The main thing was that I was startled; I already knew that you were pretty cold from seeing you in school. And I could tell that you weren't approaching me with bad intentions."

"Well, that's good, I think."

"Yes. I think it was exactly that attitude of yours, Amane, that helped make it okay... If someone you don't know suddenly treats you kindly, it's pretty scary, isn't it? Because it's scary when a stranger tries to get close."

"Sure, I guess so."

Back then, Mahiru had probably felt wary of strangers. Precisely because she had understood her own value and social standing, she'd seemed like she had drawn a definite line of separation that kept everyone else at a distance.

"Well, in the end, even though you had that kind of attitude, it did become part of the reason I felt like I could trust you, so it wasn't a bad thing."

"I'm glad it turned out that way, but, well, I still feel bad, like maybe the way I acted or what I said could have been better somehow."

Amane felt sorry he had been unfriendly, even for him, but Mahiru just smiled in amusement.

"Amane, back then, your stony face and your unfriendliness did make you stand out, you know."

"Sorry about that."

"I'm not saying it was a bad thing."

When Mahiru elegantly covered her mouth as she giggled, her soft, whisper-like laugh leaked through her fingers. Amane instinctively shot her a glare, but that only made her laugh even more, so Amane turned away in frustration.

Though she kept laughing, she didn't tease him any more than that.

Mahiru had been the one having a hard time back then, so this amount of teasing wasn't really anything to get upset about, but be that as it may, Amane didn't love it, either.

He let out a small, exasperated sigh and, as payback, ran his fingertips across her back with an expression of feigned ignorance on his face. He could feel her body jerk in surprise.

But she didn't seem inclined to reproach him for it. Instead, Mahiru got her own payback by slapping Amane, who was sitting next to her, once on the thigh.

Then she went right back to running her pen over the page of her diary. There was a distinct possibility she was recording what had just happened.

He thought she might be writing down something strange that Mahiru would tease him about later, but he had no right to stop her, so despite his complicated feelings, he pressed his lips together and simply watched Mahiru as she cheerfully wrote in her diary.

She didn't necessarily write in it every day, and she didn't necessarily fill out a whole page every time. Also, it was easy to tell by looking at it that the leather binding was fairly well-worn, so she had probably been keeping the diary for a pretty long time.

Judging by the number of pages she had made it through, about two-thirds of the way, it seemed like she'd been writing for many years. It looked like the book must have been with Mahiru the whole time she was growing up.

"Are you curious about it?"

Amane had been watching her write while trying not to look at the contents, and Mahiru seemed to have noticed his eyes on her. She tilted her head sweetly.

"Mm, it would be a lie to say I wasn't interested, but that book holds all the memories and feelings you've written down up to now, right? The good and the bad, it's all in there. If it's something that you don't want other people to see, I'm not going to force you to show me or anything."

Amane recognized that he was definitely on the possessive side, but it wouldn't be right for him to try to tell someone else what to do just because of his own feelings.

He was not going to hurt his partner just to satisfy his own curiosity, and he didn't think he needed to know every last thing about Mahiru anyway. He thought it was best for Mahiru to keep her secrets and that she would decide whether or not to tell him about them. Amane figured he didn't have the right to choose for her.

"I'm sure there are things in there you'd rather keep hidden, and it wouldn't be good for me to read them... Just because I'm your boyfriend, that doesn't mean I'm dumb or insensitive enough to go prying into your past. Plus, everyone has one or two things they'd like to keep secret."

"Amane, sometimes I don't know what to do because you're a little too understanding."

"Now, listen..."

For some reason, he felt like she was getting fed up with him, which was baffling to him, but he could tell her exasperation wasn't disapproving; instead, it tended toward admiration, so he didn't make any further complaints.

"...I'm not you, so I can't possibly know everything about you, and I'm sure there are some things I don't need to know. There's such a thing as privacy and private thoughts."

"Heh-heh, I know that, but...I just thought you might want to know, out of curiosity."

"...I don't want to go peeking over your shoulder. If you tell me something because you want me to know, that would be fine."

He would be perfectly satisfied with whatever she wanted to share. He tried to convey that he would respect her wishes to the end, but Mahiru looked like she was struggling with something as she flipped through the diary pages.

"Hmm… It's hard to pick something when you ask me about things I want to tell you."

The pages where Mahiru had recorded her life flipped past her slim fingertips, and pages lined with rounder, more youthful writing than she used now came into view and then disappeared again.

"There's not really anything all that interesting written here, you know. It's turned into less of a diary and more like a simple record, or maybe a kind of report. If you want something like a typical diary, I guess my middle school years are the closest. I was pretty emotionally immature, so whenever something bad happened, and I couldn't let it go, I wrote down my complaints in my diary, so that stuff's in there, too."

"If that's what you call immaturity, then I guess that makes people who take their anger out on everybody else babies or something."

"Well, when someone vents their anger and wants other people to cheer them up because they can't contain their own emotions, you can't deny it's a lot like a child throwing a tantrum, right?"

"That's harsh, but I guess you're right… I'll be careful."

"Why does that make you look so disheartened, Amane?"

"Oh, I was just thinking there might be a part of me that can get like that."

Amane didn't get angry much, and he didn't associate with people enough to lash out at someone else anyway, but he wondered if he only thought that was true because he had never noticed that side of himself. The people who did that kind of thing often didn't even realize what they were doing, so once again Amane cautioned himself and hoped this would be a lesson that he would not forget.

Meanwhile, Mahiru looked like she was deep in thought.

"…Amane throwing a tantrum—I'd like to see that."

"You would not!"

"I'm joking, kind of."

"Kind of?"

"I mean, it would be something new; I think it'd be cute."

"No matter how you look at it, taking out my anger on you would be psychological abuse, and I don't think there would be anything charming about it…"

Actually, it made him sick just to imagine himself throwing a tantrum and taking it out on Mahiru. It would be cute if he were a child, but while there might be a little bit of youth left in Amane's appearance, he was nearly a full-grown adult.

Surely nobody would want to see someone so old crying because things didn't go his way. And Mahiru was most likely just saying that she wanted to see Amane show more emotion rather than approving of him behaving so immaturely.

"Well, setting all that aside, it seems to me like you would be the last person to lash out at others, Amane. I mean, you're harder on yourself than anyone else, and you have a tendency to put yourself down and get depressed somewhere out of sight."

"Uh…"

"Whenever anything happens, you pretty much always think you're to blame, and you get really disheartened, right? Even when the other person is overwhelmingly in the wrong, you only pay attention to your own mistakes."

"…Well, it's rare for someone to be completely in the wrong."

Just as Mahiru said, when it came down to it, Amane was the sort of person who usually blamed himself for any problems that came up, and he often quietly beat himself up for it.

"Even if they're not one hundred percent wrong, there are definitely times when the other person is like ninety percent in the wrong, you know?"

"That's true, but—"

"I'm the same as you, but I try to be more pragmatic. I do reflect on my own behavior, but I also look objectively at whether or not I bear any of the blame, and I don't apologize or dwell on it any more than necessary. I don't want to be crushed by feelings of self-condemnation."

Amane thought it was incredible that Mahiru could think that way. It was a testament to her clear-mindedness, and he was honestly jealous she could do that.

"Well, what it comes down to is that, in the past, I was a little bit worse at processing my emotions, and it wasn't very endearing," Mahiru continued. "And I was much less adept at handling myself than I am now. I can look back on it and see how young I really was."

"Not very endearing, huh?"

"Why do you sound so doubtful?"

"Just wondering what you're counting as endearing."

Mahiru never seemed to really appreciate how adorable she was when she was talking, but she was so cute, it seemed like her behavior had to be intentional, and Amane wondered how she could say that.

Her angelic behavior, on the other hand, was something she did purposefully, so there was a part of Mahiru that expected people to think she was elegant and mature when she was acting like that. But she didn't seem conscious of her mannerisms when she was just being herself, alone with Amane, who had gotten past her whole angel persona.

Although on rare occasions she could be pushed back into that persona when agitated by someone somewhere, the rest of the time she was her true self.

Her cute gestures and word choices would have been a lot of

work for anyone else to make deliberately, but for Mahiru, they came entirely naturally, which was a scary thought.

"And who was it who once said my behavior wasn't endearing?" Mahiru asked.

"Me, though I didn't have good judgment back then."

Upon reflection, he had behaved really poorly in the past and said more than he should have. So when she pointed it out, Amane felt guilty.

"…Just like you said, Amane, I think I actually wasn't charming at all."

"But now when I think of you back then, you were super cute."

"Are you sure you're not biased because now you've fallen for me?"

"I think you were cute then even without bias, you know. Like a little hedgehog."

Now that Amane knew how she really was, when he looked back at the version of Mahiru who wouldn't relax around anyone, who had put her angel mask on and politely rejected everyone, casually refusing to allow people to approach her, she certainly seemed like a prickly little animal with lots of spikes.

Her angelic style had been her secret for protecting her mind and body, so he wasn't going to say anything about it one way or another, but looking at how relaxed and affectionate she was now, it really was hard for him to believe she was the same person.

He hadn't meant to make fun of her; rather, he thought it was an amusing and apt comparison, and he was smiling. But Mahiru, on the other hand, had puffed her cheeks like two little balloons.

Her somewhat childish expression was extremely endearing, and Amane couldn't help but comment, "Now you're a squirrel, I guess."

She delivered a series of gentle karate chops into his side.

Sure enough, she looked adorable as she smacked him, registering her complaint.

It was even cuter because Amane knew she did things like that only with him.

"...In the end, you turned into a lovely little kitten, much more docile and spoiled than you were when we first met."

"...Even though I'm not as cool as a cat anymore?"

"You did stop playing cool, didn't you?"

It would probably be more accurate to say she no longer had any need to put on an act.

She no longer had any need to keep up appearances around Amane. Precisely because she trusted Amane would accept her as she was, Mahiru let him see her in a vulnerable state.

The love that had led her to place that trust in him made him happier than anything else.

"...I don't need to act cool around you, Amane."

"You hardly ever did, even from the beginning, though."

"How terrible of me."

"Sorry for mentioning it."

"...You can apologize by petting my head, okay?"

Mahiru presented her head to him expectantly, and even as he worried he might burst out laughing, he ran his palm over her soft-looking hair.

It felt very nice to pass his fingers through the silken, flax-colored strands that were so well looked after, and just by gliding his fingers over them a little, passing right through without any snags, he caused their scent to fill the air, an invigorating yet sweet aroma.

As he carefully ran his fingers through her hair, combing through it so that it would slip through his hand with a rustling sound, Mahiru's look of displeasure quickly softened, allowing her happiness to show through.

"Does this please you, princess?"

"It does."

True to her word, Mahiru let him see her delighted expression and didn't try to hide it, and he could hardly be blamed for imagining she had grown a tail and was wagging it happily.

"Maybe you're not a cat; maybe you're a puppy dog."

"What did you say?"

"Not a thing, princess."

It seemed like he might spoil her good mood if he said too much, so he swallowed his words, tucking the thought away in his chest, then kept stroking Mahiru's head as she openly encouraged his pampering.

Mahiru seemed to have decided for the moment to pretend like she hadn't heard his comment, and she gently leaned back against him while purring and accepting the affection from his hand.

The diary was still asserting its existence in her hand.

"Don't you need to write down the next part?" he asked.

"…After we're done here, I'll write that Amane treated me like an animal again."

"If you write that, when you read it later, you're gonna think I was doing something problematic."

"Heh-heh, if I don't remember, then I'll just ask you what you were doing."

As if writing that down was already a done deal, she opened up the diary and softly ran her fingers over the unfinished passage.

"I want to make all sorts of memories going forward. I want to write them down just like the diary I've kept thus far, so they will nourish me."

Mahiru said that and flipped through the pages again, back to the past, her eyes softening as she stared nostalgically at the words written there in slightly old, somewhat faded ink.

"…I already knew this, but I can tell that when I wasn't with you, Amane, I wasn't nearly as satisfied with my life."

She didn't sound regretful or discontented or pained. Mahiru simply seemed to be thinking back with a wistful look in her eye as she told him this in a gentle tone of voice. She opened her diary to a page she must have written quite a long time ago, and she quietly closed her eyes.

Someone Similar but Different

One day, on a weekend—

The shampoo Mahiru used daily was on the verge of running out, so she went shopping for more, and while she was out, she went to the salon she always visited for a trim and a hair treatment.

She was on her way home when she stopped by a café for a rest, and she spotted a familiar face in the corner.

Since it was a weekend, there were many people in the café, so she had been looking for an open seat and ended up spotting her acquaintance. But she was unsure whether she should say anything to him.

If it had been Chitose, then Mahiru would have called out without thinking twice, but, well…although Mahiru recognized this person, Amane's friend Yuuta, he wasn't someone with whom she'd ever had much contact, so she hesitated.

I wouldn't exactly say we're close, after all.

Mahiru hadn't yet gotten a good handle on what sort of friends they were, so running into him in a café like this was awkward.

Honestly, Mahiru mostly thought of Yuuta as a friend of Amane, Itsuki, and Chitose.

Of course, when she ran into him, she was perfectly capable of talking to him normally, but if someone had asked her if Yuuta was her friend, she would have had a hard time saying yes. She still felt a little bit of distance between herself and Itsuki, after all, so that was even truer for Itsuki's friend Yuuta.

He was like a friend of a friend, and even though she knew he was not a bad person, she wouldn't exactly say they were close, either. They didn't have the kind of relationship that made her feel obligated to go out of her way to speak to him when she saw him out and about.

As she stood there, holding her tray with both hands, she wondered what to do. Then she realized she was blocking the way for the customers around her, and though she was hesitant, she walked over to the Yuuta, who was sitting at a two-person table, quietly reading a book.

"Mr. Kadowaki, good afternoon."

"Huh? Ah, Miss Shiina, hello."

She spoke to him unassumingly, and he looked up, a bit flustered, probably surprised to hear his name all of a sudden.

Since it was the weekend, Yuuta was dressed in casual clothes, and Mahiru was struck by how handsome he was. When he lifted his head, the girls around them made a bit of a commotion.

They didn't quiet down when he exchanged his expression of surprise for a gentle smile. Mahiru imagined he must have also had a hard time with that sort of thing.

"Are you out shopping today?"

"Yes, I came in here for a little rest and spotted you, Mr. Kadowaki."

She shook the shopping bag that was hanging from her wrist a little bit to show him, and Yuuta nodded in understanding.

"I see, you must be tired. Do you want to sit across from me? It doesn't look like anywhere else is open."

"Thank you very much. In that case, I will accept the seat."

Though she felt a bit shameless about it, she took him up on his kind offer and sat down in the seat across from him.

Considering the level of popularity the two of them enjoyed at school, it was probably a little risky to be sharing a table at a place like that. There was no guarantee that there weren't any other students from the same school around them.

Unfortunately, not only were there no other seats open, but when Mahiru looked around at the other tables, none of them seemed likely to become free anytime soon, so Mahiru decided it was unavoidable.

Mahiru set her tray down on the table and paused while Yuuta smiled and pulled all the loose-leaf paper spread out across the table over to his side. He had a textbook and a pen case out as well, so he had likely been studying on his own at the café.

"Mr. Kadowaki…it looks like you have a break from club activities today. Were you studying just now?"

"Yep. I thought about doing it at home, but my older sister was being annoying."

"Your sister?"

Come to think of it, she had heard from Amane in the course of conversation that Yuuta had a sister, but she was surprised to hear him say she was disruptive enough to get in the way of his studies.

She didn't know anything about his family, but she had a really hard time imagining any older sisters of Yuuta, who was so composed for a high school student and who had such a gentle disposition, would have personalities that annoyed him.

Mahiru blinked sharply several times, and Yuuta smiled wryly. "Hard to believe, huh?"

He continued, "…It isn't really something I should talk to another girl about, but… You see, when a guy has a bunch of sisters and they gang up on him, it creates this situation where he's simply no match for them. He gets overwhelmed by sheer numbers and has to listen to whatever they say…and get pushed around. A lot."

"Well, I suppose that's how some families can be."

Mahiru was, of course, an only child—though her mother had likely had another child outside of her marriage—and didn't understand the feeling of having sisters.

Or rather, she still hadn't quite grasped what a normal family was like, so she wasn't sure what kinds of roles older sisters and younger brothers would normally play. She'd heard about family hierarchies and that sort of thing, but she didn't really understand.

"I'm sure it's different for every household, but in my family, my sisters are pretty aggressive, so…"

"Heh-heh, you're a gentle and kind person, Mr. Kadowaki, so I'm sure you do all you can to grant your sisters' wishes."

"I guess you could put it that way."

"I always think it's best to phrase things in a positive light."

At any rate, it was probably true that Yuuta was annoyed by his situation, but Mahiru reasoned that even if she was agreeing with him, it wouldn't be polite to say anything negative about his sisters, so she chimed in with praise for Yuuta instead, which he answered with a slightly uncomfortable-looking expression.

She didn't sense any ill will from Yuuta toward his sisters, and they didn't seem to bother him that much, so her choice had probably been the right one.

"Well, if I stayed home, I'd get stuck doing some odd job or another, but at the same time, I wasn't feeling serious enough to go study at the library, so I came here to get a little breathing room."

"I see."

She understood what he was trying to say, but it didn't quite compute.

"Was this the right place for that?"

When she glanced at the tables around them, she could see the young women there were repeatedly looking over and talking to each other in whispers.

She wasn't interested in listening in on each and every conversation, but she figured they were probably saying something about Yuuta.

He also seemed to guess what Mahiru was implying, and he put on a thin smile.

"Mm, more or less. I'm used to that by now."

"You must have a hard time of it, too."

"Ah-ha-hah, not nearly as bad as you do."

"In that case, I have to confess that I'm used to it, too, you know?"

"Guess we both have it tough, huh?"

"We certainly do. It's a real problem."

In cases like this, Mahiru and Yuuta were two of a kind.

They would both smile bitterly if anyone mentioned it, but these two people, who were called by the nicknames *angel* and *prince*, were both good-looking individuals.

At least, they both always had to put up with the opposite sex making a fuss over them, and they both often had to deal with stares and getting chatted up. Looking at Yuuta's present situation, Mahiru reasoned he'd had similar experiences.

The main difference was that while Mahiru had deliberately been putting on her act, Yuuta was probably just being himself. He didn't seem to have a hidden side to him like she did.

"Miss Shiina, I can tell this stuff makes you uncomfortable, doesn't it?"

"Oh, but I didn't say that—"

"I didn't say anything about it, either."

"Heh-heh."

She'd always thought they had a lot in common, and now she could see their personalities were similar as well.

Yuuta probably wasn't as scheming as Mahiru was, but she also didn't believe everything about him was so neat and tidy, or that there wasn't anything about him that he kept to himself. However, it was true he was discreet about it. Mahiru smiled, willing him not to press the issue any further, and Yuuta also gave her a gentle smile.

"Well, we're never going to feel at ease as long as we keep sizing each other up like this, so let's give it a rest. Besides, I'm sure it's true you have all sorts of troubles of your own, Miss Shiina, so let's say we both have it rough and leave it at that."

"Let's do that."

Though she felt somewhat relieved Yuuta had realized it wouldn't be good to probe any further and had stopped while they were ahead, her main reaction was to reiterate to herself that she could never let her guard down.

Yuuta got along with Amane, and he was a cautious person who kept to himself, so Mahiru knew he wouldn't be a problem. And from what she had seen of him at school, she thought that, at the very least, he did have a wonderful personality.

He had kept their secret even after running into her and Amane on their date over Golden Week, and he had always treated her amicably, regardless of her angel persona, so she could tell he was a very nice person.

The fact she was still on guard was probably just a matter of habit.

Mahiru had always thought Amane was the one who was bad at getting along with other people, but maybe she was really the one who had the most trouble with it.

Because Mahiru fundamentally didn't trust other people, she had always acted the part of the angel, hanging veil upon veil to keep everyone at bay, so no matter what she did now, she probably would never come to trust Yuuta completely.

She didn't dislike him, but she didn't know him very well, and that made him a suspicious individual—was her general train of thought.

Unaware of Mahiru's internal calculations, Yuuta was looking at her with the same gentle smile as always.

"Miss Shiina, were you out with Miss Shirakawa today?"

"No, I'm on my own today. Chitose said she had plans with Mr. Akazawa, and it's not like we go out together every time anyway."

Certainly, Chitose was her closest female friend, but they didn't do everything together. Chitose, being who she was, had lots of other friends, too, so she hung out with those other girls and spent time with her boyfriend, Itsuki, as well.

Mahiru had actually heard in advance about Chitose's plans for the day, so she hadn't even asked her. Going out to buy hair care products wasn't something that was worth asking her to come along for anyway, and Mahiru was wary about intruding on Chitose's time with her boyfriend.

"Ah, Itsuki did say something about that. I just have this image of you that you're always with Miss Shirakawa."

"Heh-heh, but we haven't been hanging out all that long, you know."

"Maybe it's because she makes such a strong impression? Whenever Miss Shirakawa sees you, she rushes over shouting your name, after all."

"She sure does. She keeps me company a lot."

The friendly Chitose did things like that a lot and was always eager to see Mahiru, so it must have seemed like they were very close.

It gave people the impression they had been good friends for many years, but Mahiru had gotten to know Chitose only from the beginning of that year. In truth, not that much time had passed since they'd met.

"You look like you're such good friends, but I guess not all that much time has passed, huh? I was in a different class than either of you during our first year, so…how long have you been friends?"

"We started hanging out around the beginning of this year, I suppose."

"Ah, so it hasn't even been half a year yet."

"I'm incredibly grateful she's been spending so much time with me since then."

Even Mahiru had no clue why Chitose was so taken with her, but she had been saved time and time again by Chitose's straightforward, cheerful, friendly attitude. She was a little too energetic sometimes, but that was part of her charm.

"Miss Shirakawa seems really taken with you, Miss Shiina. I hear about you all the time from her."

"…What has Chitose been saying now? Geez…"

She'd never imagined Chitose had been talking about her to someone like Yuuta, and against her better judgment, she chided her friend even though she wasn't around to hear it.

Mahiru showed Chitose sides of herself that she would never show Yuuta, so she was incredibly worried that word of her behavior had leaked out. But Yuuta was looking at Mahiru the same way he always did, so she wanted to believe Chitose hadn't put any funny ideas in his head.

Mahiru internally resolved to caution Chitose casually about her big mouth later as she sipped her mostly cooled café au lait. But Yuuta was watching her intently with a gentle look in his eyes.

"…It's surprisingly easy to talk to you, you know."

"What do you mean?"

She answered him with a question after moistening her lips, and Yuuta was evasive for a moment. "Hmm, how can I put this?"

Then he said, "Well, this is kind of strange for me to say, but it's not like you're particularly good friends with me, right? To you, I'm probably more like a friend of a friend, and given that relationship, I assumed we'd have a hard time striking up a conversation."

Mahiru hadn't even considered that Yuuta himself might have been anxious about the same things. After she blinked dramatically several times, she noticed he had an apprehensive, awkward, and uncertain look in his eye, and he was wearing a soft smile, so that made the little bit of wariness that had welled up inside her settle back down.

"Well, it would be a lie to say I wasn't reluctant at all, but I think I know you well enough, Mr. Kadowaki, so…"

"I'm so happy you approve of me. I was sure you didn't care for me very much, Miss Shiina."

"Didn't care for you?"

"Ah, maybe that's not quite it, more like, you were avoiding me because you thought it might be a hassle to associate with me maybe?"

Mahiru should have expected as much, but Yuuta was an intelligent person who was sensitive to the opinions and attention of others.

Both she and Yuuta had resisted getting close to one another because they were each certain it would only cause trouble. Of course, she was not interested in him, so the biggest reason was that getting involved with him seemed like it would attract unwanted attention.

If the two of them—Mahiru, who was so popular with the boys, and Yuuta, who was so popular with the girls—started getting along, it wasn't hard to imagine the tidal wave of jealousy that would sweep over them. It would certainly cause both of them a headache, even more so than usual.

Mahiru wouldn't have even considered sitting with Yuuta like this if he wasn't already friends with Amane. And Yuuta must have likewise decided not to invite any trouble, and to keep his distance out of a desire not to add any unnecessary anxiety to their lives.

It must have been precisely because Yuuta also understood the stakes that he'd never made contact, even though they'd both been given similarly embarrassing nicknames. Though for Mahiru, the idea that, just like her, he simply wasn't interested in her had some appeal.

"I see. I can certainly see why you would be apprehensive about that, but that still doesn't give me a reason to dislike you on a personal level, Mr. Kadowaki."

"...I guess that's true."

"I think both of us were keeping an appropriate amount of distance, given that strange rumors would start flying if we didn't, but I never particularly thought about you one way or another is the thing."

She was most definitely staying slightly on guard and thinking she couldn't get too comfortable around him. But she didn't find his personality unpleasant, and if anything, she thought he was just the type of person that she liked.

At least, as far as chatting went, Mahiru found Yuuta pleasant enough despite her misanthropic tendencies.

"Thanks very much for that."

"Actually, I thought you were the one who had a negative opinion of me, Mr. Kadowaki."

"That's not true at all."

"I'm glad to hear that, but..."

She knew he'd also been avoiding her, because of their popularity. But Yuuta's attitude hadn't ever changed all that much, even when other people weren't watching them. Also, sometimes it felt like he was a little awkward around her, so she'd thought there might be some reticence toward her from his side.

His frowning eyebrows told her she hadn't exactly hit the nail on the head, but she'd said something he wasn't expecting, and now he wasn't sure what to say. She was once again aware she had misunderstood something, and she sighed quietly.

"By the way, is it okay for you to sit here having coffee with me?"

"What?"

She received this curious question while she sat there lamenting that she still had some maturing to do.

She answered him in her natural tone of voice, and he looked startled, so Mahiru cleared her throat and asked again, "What do you mean by that?"

Yuuta put on a troubled smile that was different than the one he had on earlier. "I mean, do you have to hurry over…back to Fuji…to that guy's place? I'm wondering if you could stay for a while."

He had avoided saying Amane's name, mostly out of consideration for their surroundings.

But Mahiru would have preferred he hadn't asked in the first place. The question almost made her spill the café au lait she was nursing.

She looked carefully up at Yuuta, trying not to let him sense how shaken she was, and she saw that, for some reason, he was wearing a puzzled expression.

"Wh-what gave you that sort of idea?"

"Uh, you're always together, right?"

"Wh-why—"

"I mean, I can tell just by looking at you guys… Given the way you behave, it's obvious to anyone who sees you. You're together all the time, so…"

She had already explained to Yuuta she'd been going over to Amane's apartment to make meals, and he understood they were very close, but she hadn't expected to hear he thought they were always together.

Sure, Mahiru was often at Amane's place. She hung out there so often she now thought of it as her own home, and she spent her time there even outside of meal times.

Amane had never prevented her from doing so and had always accepted her presence, so it had become normal for her, but it was a big shock to have it pointed out by someone a little further removed.

And then, to have it pointed out again that people knew just how much she loved Amane, made Mahiru nearly groan in distress. She only barely managed to maintain her composure. She decided not to dwell on whether she was really managing to keep up appearances.

"...I'm really not...o-over there every day."

"But you're over there pretty frequently. You seem to go about six times a week."

"I won't deny that. After all, we split our groceries, so that means we eat most meals together."

"So it's only reasonable you'd be together, huh?" Yuuta nodded earnestly.

Mahiru had already dropped her reserved demeanor and glared at him just a little with her natural expression.

"...Is there something you'd like to say to me, Mr. Kadowaki?"

"Ah, there's not anything in particular I'd like to say, but... ummm, if I have to say something, it's that you're much more animated now than you are when I see you in school."

"Isn't everyone like that when they're among friends?"

"But it also seems different than when you're with Miss Shirakawa."

Mahiru couldn't say anything in response to that. Instead, she pressed her lips together. As if to set her at ease, Yuuta waved his hand lightly, with a soft look in his eye.

"I'm not trying to tell you how to live your life or anything. I simply wondered if it wouldn't be better for you to spend your time with him instead of me. He won't get jealous?"

Apparently he was trying to express his concern in his own way, but the stress made Mahiru's heart skip a beat. She would have liked for him to just stop talking.

...Jealous? Never.

Actually, Amane never got jealous of the people around Mahiru. That was how his personality had always been; he wasn't one to feel jealousy toward people who had nothing to do with him.

The one getting jealous was always Mahiru.

"...It would be easier on me if he did actually get jealous, I think," she admitted.

"Ah-ha-ha!"

"If you were in his position, do you think you would get jealous, Mr. Kadowaki?"

"Hmm, it's kind of a strange question to bring up, but I don't think I would get jealous. And I think if I told him you'd gone out for coffee with me, he'd pretty much shrug it off."

"...You know him very well."

"Has anything like that ever happened?"

"I've talked with Mr. Akazawa before, just the two of us. But he was much more suspicious I might have said something out of line than he was jealous or anything."

"That sounds just like him."

"Though it's good he doesn't really get jealous of other people."

"If anything, it seems like you're the one who gets worked up about things, Miss Shiina."

Faced with someone who seemed to read everything that was

on her mind, Mahiru thought that perhaps Yuuta was someone she couldn't handle after all... That was how it made her feel.

Yuuta was totally unlike Amane, who was surprisingly frank and honest in spite of how calm he usually was, or Itsuki, who was oddly perceptive despite joking around all the time. Yuuta kept his thoughts concealed behind a smile, and he was shrewd, the type of boy who could be trouble if you made an enemy of him.

Though Itsuki was also someone she didn't quite mesh with, his obvious loyalty to Amane explained his behavior and helped her accept him—even if it was hard for her to decipher his thoughts at times.

She turned a probing eye on him, but when her gaze fell on Yuuta, he gave a nervous chuckle. "I'm sorry, I wasn't trying to poke fun at you. I just meant to say that it's easy to tell you're deeply involved with him, that's all."

"...Is it that obvious?"

"Yeah."

When he agreed instantly, she put a hand to her cheek and sighed softly.

"I guess we'll have to be more careful. It's not good to be so obvious yet."

"Not yet, huh?"

"Yes, not yet."

"Then I hope the right time comes for you soon."

Perhaps because of Mahiru's suspicions, it sounded to her like there was a hidden meaning behind his words, but Yuuta himself probably meant it as a genuine expression of support. She was perfectly aware of her habit of regarding others with suspicion, so she tried not to make too much of it.

Be that as it may, his thoughts were still hard to read, so she narrowed her eyes a little and said, "...This is rude of me to say when you're right here in front of me, but has anyone ever told you it's hard to tell what you're thinking?"

"Don't people often say that about you, too?"

"Heh-heh, they do, behind my back."

Indeed, Mahiru wasn't in a position to be criticizing Yuuta.

When she put on her angel mask, Mahiru was kind and polite to everyone. However, she knew some people didn't appreciate her goody-two-shoes act, and they talked behind her back about how her beauty was only skin-deep. There was nothing she could do about that.

Mahiru was used to people bad-mouthing her. For all the praise she got from other people, she also had to endure an enormous amount of jealousy, envy, and resentment.

People had started whispering behind her back after she'd settled into her angel persona, but that didn't mean there weren't some people who deliberately let her overhear them insulting her when she was alone.

She understood that the more brilliant she was, the stronger her light shined, and the deeper the shadows it would create.

For exactly that reason, she had never tried to do anything about that negative aspect of things, and she'd never expected it to change.

Without letting her expression slip, and without saying a word, she just smiled back at Yuuta, trying to express that she was used to that treatment by now, and she had accepted it as a part of life.

Yuuta had been smiling, but his expression clouded over.

"So you know they're talking, huh?"

"Yes."

"...I feel like you've got it harder than I do, really."

"I'm used to it."

Really, it was probably not good for her to grow accustomed to such things, but it had become far too ordinary, and she considered it part of her everyday life. It had become commonplace.

"Well, don't pay it any mind. Or what I mean to say is, I wouldn't know what to do if they came after me."

"I'm not foolish enough to pour oil on the fire."

"Thank you for your discretion."

Mahiru was grateful Yuuta stopped there, considering his own popularity.

He also seemed to understand perfectly well it took more than a sense of justice for things to turn out all right.

"Before things get too difficult, you'd better have a proper conversation with your man," he said.

"You might be right. I'll give it some thought."

She accepted Yuuta's advice, but as long as things didn't get too bad, she didn't intend to turn to Amane for help.

Even so, she was grateful she had someone to turn to, and she could tell Yuuta's recommendation came from a place of concern, so Mahiru nodded and then finished the rest of her café au lait, which had gone completely cold.

After parting from Yuuta and finishing some additional shopping, Mahiru went home, or more accurately, she went back to Amane's place. It was early evening, and she saw he had diligently set about preparations for dinner, which filled her chest with a steady warmth.

Amane was doing his best preparing the vegetables while looking at the recipe Mahiru had left for him. Apparently he hadn't noticed her come in, as he was busily running around the kitchen on his own.

She watched him measuring things and staring down at the recipe, rustling the apron he had only recently started wearing as he worked, and her overwhelming love for him made her mouth curl into a smile.

"I just got back."

When she called out to Amane, who was working so diligently, she saw him jump.

He turned smoothly toward her, and the moment their eyes met, Mahiru grinned and Amane frowned apologetically.

"Ah, welcome home. Sorry, I was concentrating, and I didn't hear you come in."

"I bet you were. I can tell just by looking!"

She had absolutely no intention of criticizing him; in fact, it tickled her when she saw Amane had started getting dinner ready on his own, and instead of being annoyed, she was filled with feelings of delight and happiness.

"You really could have waited until I got home. I sent you a message saying I was on the way, you know?"

"I wasn't looking at my phone, sorry. But it makes it easier on you if I do all this first, right?"

When Amane smiled and said he'd figured prep would take some time that day because some ingredients needed to be pickled, an indescribably ticklish and happy feeling welled up inside her.

Though he had initially left all the cooking up to Mahiru, Amane had started regularly lending a hand and had even started cooking on his own, thinking ahead like this. Amane's growth was amazing. If the Amane from six months earlier could see him now, his legs would go out from under him.

"Thank you very much," she said softly to Amane, who had been incredibly thoughtful so she could enjoy her outing.

Amane looked amused. "That's usually my line, you know."

Thinking about how that was one of the things she loved about him, she set her purchases down on the sofa. Then she tied up her hair and went back to the kitchen, where Amane was working, only to see Amane staring at her for some reason.

"Is something wrong?"

"No, your hair's just even silkier than usual today. I mean, it's always silky, but it's, like, particularly glossy or something."

"...Did I tell you where I was going today, Amane?"

She'd told him she was going out shopping, but she didn't think she'd said anything about going to the hair salon.

If he had known she was going to the salon, he would have expected to see a difference in her hair. But without knowing about her visit, he could have known only by observing her very closely.

Mahiru never failed to look after her hair on a regular basis, so getting hair care at a salon didn't change anything dramatically. The quality of her hair was better than usual, but if anything, it was an improvement only in the texture.

"Huh? No, I didn't want to pry, so I didn't ask where. It's just, when you were putting it up just now, it seemed a little neater than usual or, like, real smooth and pretty."

"You're almost unbelievably observant."

"...Ah, so you went to the salon? That makes sense."

He seemed to grasp where she had gone that day after she confirmed her hair quality had improved, and he praised her without getting too carried away. "It looks pretty."

Mahiru refused to meet his eyes and quietly muttered. "Thank you very much."

Amane didn't seem to take any particular notice of the change in Mahiru's expression. As he looked at the recipe stuck to the refrigerator, he chuckled. "I think it's about time I go, too."

She wasn't sure whether she should be impressed by Amane casually voicing his awareness of that fact, or whether she should complain that it was so typical of him. Mahiru kept her mouth shut as she wondered, her heart pounding strangely as she stood next to Amane, washing her hands.

While she appreciated the sight of Amane, who had totally gotten used to cooking, performing the prep work perfectly, Mahiru checked the next step in the recipe and then peered into the refrigerator.

"Did you have fun on your outing?"

In response to his question, coming softly from off to the side, Mahiru smiled slightly.

"Yes, sometimes it's nice to go walk about on my own."

"That's great. It seems like you haven't been going out much lately."

"Well, I'm really more of an indoor person, so I don't go out unless I've got an errand to run, you know. I guess I don't really have much energy for finding reasons to go out."

"Ha-ha, I get that. I also don't go out without a good reason."

"You'd prefer to watch a movie or play a game at home, wouldn't you, Amane?"

"Right, right, I'm more laid-back."

Amane was even more of an indoor type than Mahiru was, but on his days off, he didn't stay locked inside all day. Instead, he hung out with Itsuki and the other boys or went for a run.

The boys tended to do fairly active things when they hung out, too, so he wasn't necessarily a total couch potato.

"By the way, I ran into Mr. Kadowaki today. We talked for a little while."

"Did you? I guess there weren't any club activities today. What was he up to?"

"…You were right."

Of course, Mahiru's words weren't for Amane, but instead directed at someone who wasn't there.

"It's kind of a strange question to bring up, but I don't think I would get jealous. And I think if I told him you'd gone out for coffee with me, he'd pretty much shrug it off."

She recalled what Yuuta had said at the café and realized Amane had just responded exactly as Yuuta had predicted. It made her feel weirdly frustrated somehow.

"Hm, what's up?"

"Nothing. I just happened to run across him while he was studying at a café, and we shared a table; that's all. He said his sisters would push him around if he went home."

"Ha-ha, I've heard they can be a handful. It must be really terrible, for Kadowaki to say something."

As his friend, Amane knew more about Yuuta than Mahiru did, but he didn't seem to have actually met Yuuta's sisters, and he was smiling in amusement as he imagined it.

"...Is something wrong?"

Amane must have noticed Mahiru was lost in thought, and he spoke to her in a tone of concern, so she shook her head slowly.

"...How do I put this...? Mr. Kadowaki is someone I can't let out of my sight, I think."

"Did Kadowaki do something?"

"No, it's just, since we're similar types of people...when we were together, there was this strange tension in the air..."

There was no way she could say she thought there was something shady about Yuuta, so she was deliberately ambiguous, and she softened what she had felt that day as she described it to Amane.

Amane seemed more or less convinced and signaled his understanding, "Ah, like you were feeling each other out?"

"We both have our reputations to consider, so I'm sure we did it automatically, but it was still scary."

"Sure, I get that, but Kadowaki's a good guy, for sure."

"I know that! It's just, people who are unconditionally nice scare me. People who do things that have no merit for them personally are harder to deal with than those who are after some reward."

Without a doubt, Yuuta was a good person.

He was the type of person who naturally made Mahiru suspicious, but she could tell he wasn't a bad person. Although he was difficult to read, she believed he was a decent guy.

But for Mahiru, who had gone through her life without letting anyone get close, putting her full trust in him was a step too far.

She knew he was thoughtful and he had a keen personality and he had been very supportive about her relationship with Amane. But she still found herself trying to read into his hidden side, without even knowing whether or not he had one.

"I understand what you're trying to say, but I don't think you really need to be on your guard so much about that."

"I already know that, but…"

It was in Mahiru's nature to be vigilant anyway.

"Well, if he's not your cup of tea, I don't think you have to force yourself to hang out with him. I wonder if I should watch myself a little around him, too?"

"Oh, no, I didn't mean to say that I dislike him. But…"

"But?"

"…He just…gives me pause."

For some reason, the high degree to which Yuuta understood Amane gave her a bad feeling.

As far as Mahiru knew, Amane and Yuuta had been hanging out only since the start of the new year, so she was surprised he had developed such an accurate picture of Amane in such a short time. And even though she knew Amane didn't belong to her, she felt like Yuuta had usurped her position as the person who understood Amane best, and it really bothered her.

"You get a bad feeling about him?"

"I don't know if it's bad exactly… I'm just being selfish. I don't dislike him or anything like that."

"All right. Well, some people just don't have chemistry. There's no helping that."

"But...it's like, you know, Mister Kadowaki knows you really well, for no real reason."

Amane cocked his head curiously at her.

"He does?"

"He does."

"...Why are you sulking?"

"I'm not sulking."

As she added the seasonings Amane had apparently measured out in advance to the pot, Mahiru tried to convince herself she was not feeling even the tiniest bit jealous of Yuuta.

Rome Wasn't Built in a Day

Amane knew Mahiru was a hardworking person, someone who never allowed herself to compromise.

People who didn't know her very well tended to think she was some sort of genius, someone who was quick to understand everything, but from Amane's perspective, she just seemed like a bright person who added effort on top of the talent she already possessed as she acquired more knowledge and experience.

And that wasn't limited to book smarts. When it came to athletic ability, beauty, housework, and everything else, Mahiru had mastered them all after much effort, and Amane knew none of them had been half-hearted endeavors.

"…Mahiru's such a hardworking person," he mumbled as he gazed at her. She was lifting a light dumbbell as she listened to her English study materials.

He had thought she was focused on her task, but apparently Mahiru had heard him, because she glanced over in his direction.

Even as she looked at him, she continued her weight training with the dumbbell. He realized it must have been exercises like this that maintained her slender, supple upper arms.

"I'm glad you see me that way…I guess?"

"Why was that a question?"

"Well, there are some people who would say it's more virtuous to hide your hard work."

With a laugh, she added that she did all her hard work right there in front of Amane's eyes, and she then paused the recording she had been playing. Amane looked at her in disbelief.

"No way. What's wrong with showing people you're working hard?"

"Maybe it's the idea you're showing off your effort or something?"

"It might be kind of a problem if you are really flaunting it, but there can't be any issue with someone trying hard. I bet the people who say it's a virtue to hide your effort would also look down on your accomplishments if you only showed them the results. They'd be, like, anyone can do that."

People would insist that since another person was able to do something without any trouble, it must be an easy task, while ignoring all the effort and time and money and everything else the other person put into acquiring their skills. It was sad but often true.

"Well, it's not like I'm hiding anything; it's just that people don't see the things I always do at home, right?" Mahiru said easily.

Then she mumbled the number fifteen, lowered the dumbbell onto the carpet, and lightly touched her own upper arm, gently checking on its condition.

It was just as she said. Mahiru did her work at home…or actually, at Amane's home, and no one other than he ever saw her like this. They didn't know about it, so some made light of all the work that she did.

The fact she didn't seem to mind what others thought might have been because she was extremely open-minded, or because she was used to people saying things they shouldn't.

"I act serious at school, but it's not like I'm totally devoted to studying, so, well, I guess sometimes being able to study seems like a talent."

"It probably is a kind of talent, but in the end, it's your efforts that make things blossom. After all, the degree of effort you put in is on another level, Mahiru... I think it's easy to see you're diligent."

"Once I make it a habit, it becomes second nature, and the mental load feels lighter, you see. Besides, I get results in proportion to how much effort I put in, which I recognize is a blessing. So from an outsider's point of view, that makes me look talented, and I want to capitalize on that the best I can."

Mahiru was continually working on improving herself, but she was also realistic about her efforts, and she could evaluate her progress honestly, without getting anxious or worked up. She looked so confident and composed Amane was almost enchanted.

"After all, I originally started all this to become the good girl my parents wanted, but now instead of an objective like that, I put in all this effort simply to improve myself. Surprisingly, I don't find it difficult, physically or mentally."

"You work harder than anyone I know, seriously."

"Well, I'm doing it all for my future, after all."

"...For your future?"

"Yes, my future."

Mahiru put on a beautiful smile and peered directly into Amane's eyes.

"Amane, everybody gets old, you know."

"Huh, what's this all of a sudden?"

She'd jumped to a topic he never would have anticipated. Amane was flustered. He didn't understand what she meant. But Mahiru didn't seem to pay any attention, and she continued right along.

"People age. Just like beautiful flowers in full bloom eventually wither, with every year humans age, we lose the beauty and physical abilities we had when we were young."

That was just the law of nature.

There was variation among living things, but they all aged with time, moving toward death. Once something was past its physical prime, the more years that piled on, the more bodily functions declined and looks faded.

"Amane, I'm very good-looking and cute, right?"

A broad grin would probably be the right way to describe the smile she gave him, full of charm and confidence. Anyone who'd seen it would probably have called it cute, just like she said.

Coming from anyone else, that question might have sounded conceited, but Amane didn't find it disagreeable in the least, because she *was* good-looking, and on top of that, her efforts had shaped every aspect of her appearance, from the top of her head to the tips of her toes, and he knew it.

When it came to her flaxen hair, soft and glossy like silk, Mahiru was constantly looking after it, combing it so it wouldn't get tangled, using all sorts of different shampoos and treatments and conditioners on it.

The same went for her skin. He knew she paid incredible attention to her skin care products and never failed to moisturize diligently, and he also understood that by eating meals with a good nutritional balance, she was taking care of her skin from the inside out.

He also knew her lean, firm, and yet feminine figure was something she had built through careful diet and vigilant exercise.

Probably precisely because he lived alongside her, he knew how much time and labor Mahiru spent on her looks, and precisely because he had seen her process, he found Mahiru's words very persuasive.

"You're incredibly beautiful. I think it's the result of all your efforts."

Mahiru had nice features to begin with, and that was likely thanks to genetics and not to anything she'd done.

However, she possessed a beauty that DNA alone couldn't explain, which wouldn't have come out if she hadn't constantly polished herself. Amane knew better than anyone how much work Mahiru had put in.

When he spoke from the heart after wavering a little over how he ought to compliment her, that smile of Mahiru's took on a bashful shade and became even softer.

"Thank you very much. I work really hard at it."

"I know you do; you're always working hard."

He had come to spend a lot of time by Mahiru's side and had been able to see all of her efforts.

Mahiru was smiling bashfully, and her cheeks had flushed faintly, perhaps out of embarrassment from Amane's compliment. But then she coughed to clear her throat and pulled herself together to continue.

"But I'm only going to be this cute at my present age. As a general rule, people prefer youth, right?"

"I understand what you're trying to say, but—"

"Of course, I'm taking care I don't immediately wither away, but eventually, I'm going to get old. And if you depend on such unreliable things…I don't think the world is forgiving enough to let you get by with just good looks and charm."

Mahiru, who had quite a severe way of thinking, let out a soft sigh and then looked at him.

"Even supposing it was possible, I don't think I'd want to do that. It's too risky. I might incur the world's wrath, after all."

"Uh…well, I guess you wouldn't want to deliberately cross such a dangerous bridge."

"Even under normal circumstances, even in my present position, people are already pretty jealous of me, so I just hate the idea of attracting even worse jealousy. Already people make a fuss over me just from seeing my face, and it's really annoying."

Even though, as a basic rule, Mahiru didn't boast or draw attention to the fact she was beautiful, still there were people who envied her for getting showered with affection from men.

She didn't face much undisguised jealousy or criticism, thanks to the way she conducted herself as the angel, plus her natural talents and her sociable attitude. But if Mahiru ever did use her good looks to her advantage, it was clear as day what would happen.

Mahiru hated getting attention from total strangers, so just by her nature, she would definitely never do that, but if she ever did, both the boys and the girls would be upset.

Mahiru herself seemed to understand that, too, and was wearing a weary expression as if she was imagining it.

"…Well, what I mean to say is it's also important to improve yourself on the inside and develop your skills. Because in the future, even if I'm attractive, that won't be worth anything, and it won't help me as an adult, and so I want to avoid getting judged based on my looks, you see?"

Mahiru brought her argument to a close with this incredibly pragmatic opinion and turned a calm smile on Amane, who was bewildered by how secure she was in her thoughts.

"When someone is old and all their beauty falls away, what comes seeping out from the inside is the record of the life that person lived, their real substance, I think. I want to live my life in a way that doesn't make me ashamed of who I am."

"That's definitely not a normal way for a high school student to think…"

"Heh-heh. I've always been like this, because I was educated by Miss Koyuki."

This time Mahiru smiled impishly, and Amane wanted to make a quip about what a weird person this Koyuki must have been. Miss Koyuki's teachings must have formed the basis for the strength of character Mahiru had now, and they were definitely her guiding principles.

He could imagine she had probably been concerned about Mahiru, and so she had made sure Mahiru saw the world as it was.

Amane wasn't sure whether it had been the right decision to teach her about how harsh reality could be.

However, it must have been thanks to Miss Koyuki's influence that Mahiru didn't despair about her future and instead had developed the kind of personality and way of thinking that allowed her to put in the effort to live a strong life.

"Anyway, this is kind of a difficult thing to express, but I want to become a person with genuine depth, is what I'm saying. Because if I live my life only keeping up appearances and never thinking much of anything, then when my time is up, I'd probably regret how I spent my days."

"I understand what you're trying to say, but I can't believe you thought it through that far."

Mahiru raised her eyebrows a little and smiled at Amane.

He was feeling both admiration toward Mahiru, who had laid out her case so well it was like she had seen the future and was living her life for the second time, as well as loathing toward himself for having never thought that far ahead.

"You're not shocked or repulsed? Even I think I have a flawed character."

"No, not at all, but I just haven't thought that far ahead, is all. Just makes me feel a little pathetic, I guess."

"Why would that make you feel pathetic?"

"I've been working hard to improve my present situation, but I've never even considered setting my eyes that far in the future and working toward something like that."

Amane was also making efforts, but they weren't as comprehensive as Mahiru's, and he didn't have any particularly clear objectives.

He had started everything out of a desire to be able to stand by Mahiru's side with pride.

Of course, Amane was working hard in his own way, and the results of his work were starting to show, but thinking about the amount of effort that he put in, he wasn't working nearly as hard as she was, and he hadn't set such strict goals for himself, so it seemed presumptuous for him to compare himself to her.

He'd been told to stop being so self-abasing, and he was trying to be careful about it, but still, since he was able to see Mahiru's tenacity up close, he felt disappointed by the difference between them.

"Why is it you're comparing yourself to me like that?"

"Sorry."

"What do you need to apologize for? It's wonderful you're working hard to improve yourself! All your efforts matter. The work you're doing now will pay off in the future, you'll see. And it's okay to admit to yourself that you're doing a good job right now."

Mahiru smacked his cheeks with the pads of her fingers. She peered at him with an exasperated smile and a chiding look in her eye.

"...Okay."

"You really don't have any confidence, do you, Amane?"

"I—I can't help it, can I? I mean, I'm not even sure if I've been honest with myself about everything..."

"You decided aspects of yourself were lacking, and you are putting in the effort to fix them now, aren't you? Isn't that proof that you're doing just fine?"

"I'd like to think so, but…wahh!"

When Amane failed to agree with her, Mahiru put her hands on Amane's cheeks and, without hesitation, pinched them between her fingers.

Even though Amane didn't have a lot of fat there to begin with, there was more than enough for her fingers to dig in. His cheeks were firmer than Mahiru's and not as easy to stretch, but she still pulled them out far enough to make it hard for him to talk.

"Hey, howd on—"

"…If you won't admit to any more than that, then your punishment is for me to squish your cheeks until you recognize how well you're doing."

"I—I ged da point…"

"Great."

She seemed satisfied but didn't show any signs of letting him go. Amane stared at her.

"…Wet me go, pwease."

"…I can't hold on a little longer?"

"Nobe."

"Hmph."

For some reason, Mahiru had settled into a combination of kneading one of Amane's cheeks while rubbing the other one. She reluctantly pulled her hands away, and Amane clutched his face, feeling like it was more elastic than before.

It didn't hurt, but it was kind of a strange sensation.

For some reason, she was still looking at him wistfully, but she stopped immediately when Amane chided her. "Now look here…"

Somehow or other, Mahiru occasionally found a reason to touch Amane and enjoy being in contact with him, either because she simply liked touching him or because she liked to tease him. Since he was the one on the receiving end, it was very hard for Amane to stay calm when she did.

Amane finally managed to dispel the uncomfortable feeling in his cheeks and his heart, which had been pounding at a faster rate than usual, so he turned to face Mahiru again, and the impish side of her she'd been showing him until a moment earlier vanished into thin air, and she put on a gentle smile that was calm and enveloping.

"...Amane, you're working really hard."

Her voice, which was much calmer and more compassionate than even her expression, slid right into Amane's ears.

"I won't say you don't have anything to work on, but you're aware of your shortcomings, and you are actively trying to improve yourself. If there's anyone who wants to complain about that, I'll punish them myself."

"You don't need to dirty your hands, Mahiru."

"Trust me, I'll do a good job with just my words, okay?"

"That'll just make your mouth dirty."

"Don't worry, I'm not about to say anything *too* outrageous."

"No, I think we're good."

Mahiru, who was grinning at him with her perfect smile, obviously gave off the sense she hated conflict, and yet she was always true to her word.

Since she would definitely do something once she put her mind to it, Amane was fairly certain if he didn't stop her, she would argue any opponent into a corner until they surrendered, with a smile on her face. She never got angry when people criticized her, and yet when it came to Amane, she would get worked up like she was defending herself; more, even. Amane wasn't sure whether to be glad or upset by it.

But for the time being, any criticisms he might receive were only hypothetical, so Amane put a hold on the subject, since there was no point in her getting angry about it just then. Mahiru looked unsatisfied, so he ruffled her hair to distract her.

Mahiru resisted a little bit, probably because she knew when she got patted on the head, he was trying to make her shake off her negative emotions, but ultimately, she seemed to like getting her head stroked, and she obediently accepted Amane's hand.

Once her anger at her fictional opponent had subsided after a few moments of soothing by Amane's palm, Mahiru grumbled, "Geez, I'm not even really angry."

The way she was acting, she looked like a pouting child, and that wasn't Amane's imagination.

She gave him another reluctant look when he removed his hand after she had completely settled down, but he didn't think it was good to go on touching her for too long, so he intentionally ignored it.

"…I'm not really all that interested in getting approval from everybody, I guess."

"You're not?"

"I mean, I do want the people around me to accept me, of course, but…it's more like I want to satisfy myself. I just feel like I have to become a version of myself that I can be proud of."

Amane had never particularly cared for the idea of winning the approval of some unspecified crowd of people.

He wanted to feel worthy of standing by Mahiru's side, and that was more of a battle with himself than with anyone else. Though he was often painfully aware of the distance between his goals and his reality, he never worried about the judgments of others.

Above anyone else, the person he had to convince of his worth was himself and no one else.

He was glad to get recognition from others that he had changed, but that was not his objective.

"…I see. Well then, I'll keep watch over you so you can get the results you want, Amane."

"I'll try my best. For my own sake," Amane said resolutely.

After gazing at him in wonderment for a moment, Mahiru nodded with a faint flush on her cheeks. "I'm rooting for you," she whispered, and laughed as she patted Amane on the back.

Fleeting Dreams and Cruelties of Youth

Sitting at the dining table, which made a satisfying sound as she rhythmically tapped on it, Mahiru was cheerfully completing her homework.

Mahiru generally did her homework in her own room, but on the days when Miss Koyuki came, she often worked at the dining table while listening to the sounds of Miss Koyuki cooking.

Honestly, it was simple for Mahiru to get through something as easy as her homework, but sitting there at the table like that, leisurely doing her homework while she listened to the sounds from the kitchen—knives chopping, ingredients sizzling in the pan, gentle simmering—and smelling the aroma wafting out was the thing she loved most of all.

Besides, Mahiru knew if she sat at the table, Miss Koyuki would see how hard she was working, and she would praise her.

Mahiru happily worked away at her homework, aware Miss Koyuki was looking in to check on her from time to time.

She worked ever so slowly, to make it last until Miss Koyuki had finished cooking.

Though Mahiru was hungry, she enjoyed this time, and she

hoped it would last even longer. It was worth being hungry to spend more time with Miss Koyuki.

"Young lady, your supper's ready."

"Okay!"

After a little while, Mahiru heard the voice she had been waiting for and called back excitedly as she rushed to close the notebook that had been open on the table.

Though she had tried to delay reaching the end of her assignment, she had already completed it, so she couldn't keep pretending she was working on it to get praise, but since she was finished, she would probably get praised anyway. Mahiru smiled modestly to herself.

If she didn't clean up properly, Miss Koyuki would scold her when she came to set dinner out, so Mahiru carefully gathered up all of her eraser crumbs and threw them away in the trash can, then collected her notebook filled with scrawled numbers, as well as her numerous printouts, and set them on the living room table.

Then she entered the kitchen with a smile, just as Miss Koyuki was taking off her apron, wearing a gentle smile of her own.

"You worked hard at your homework again today, didn't you?"

"Yes."

As always, she had been watching Mahiru.

The woman who filled two roles as both housekeeper and governess kept a gentle smile on her face as she folded her apron and whispered to Mahiru, "Go and wash your hands, and I'll set out your dinner."

Unhesitatingly, Mahiru nodded and went over to the sink. As she stood on her tiptoes washing her hands, she glanced over at the numerous dishes being arranged on the dining table, and she smiled.

Apparently the day's menu was Japanese-style food.

The rest of Mahiru's family didn't think much of Japanese food, but Mahiru herself loved the taste. She liked Western-style food, too, but personally she thought Japanese food was more comforting and reassuring.

Miss Koyuki always said, "You need to taste all sorts of different things and develop your palate while you're still young," and she made a variety of different foods for Mahiru. But Mahiru's absolute favorite were the Japanese-style meals.

After washing her hands thoroughly, Mahiru went to the table. Miss Koyuki sat down across from her.

There was no meal for Miss Koyuki.

Though Mahiru wished just once they could eat a meal together, Miss Koyuki was, after all, just the "housekeeper," and not family.

Since Miss Koyuki always declined while sounding restrained and apologetic, Mahiru felt like she ate all of her meals alone.

I wish we could eat together.

However, she knew whining selfishly about it would put Miss Koyuki in an awkward spot, so she never voiced this desire.

As she let out a secret little sigh, she admired the dishes on the table.

That day, a perfect Japanese meal had been arranged for her, including the usual rice and miso soup, as well as rolled dashi omelets, stewed chicken and vegetables, and boiled spinach dressed in sesame sauce.

"It looks yummy."

"I made everything to the best of my ability, as always. Eat please, before it gets cold."

"Okay."

Mahiru nodded, put her hands together, and politely intoned, "Thank you for the meal," then quietly took a sip of miso soup.

The soup's warmth gradually sank into her insides, and the mild, comforting flavor was Mahiru's absolute favorite. Whenever she

©Hanekoto

drank this soup, she had the sensation of being pleasantly warmed from the inside out, and it made her happy.

Everything was so delicious that Mahiru silently chewed away, bringing her meal to her mouth bite by bite, while Miss Koyuki watched over her with a cheerful grin.

"Miss Koyuki, why are you so good at cooking?"

After she had finished eating, while she was helping Miss Koyuki clear away the dishes, Mahiru asked the question that had been weighing on her mind.

Miss Koyuki's cooking was incredibly tasty. Mahiru knew it was bad to compare it to her school lunches, but she thought it was wonderful how Miss Koyuki prepared so many more things that were to Mahiru's taste than they did at school.

"Well, let's see, it must be because I've been alive several times longer than you, young lady, and I made meals for my daughters every day. When you're a mother to children, you naturally become good at things like that."

"So then, does that mean my mother is good at cooking, too?"

It was a simple question, but the moment she asked it, it caused Miss Koyuki's smile to stiffen.

But she soon reverted to her usual gentle expression and turned to Mahiru with a kind look in her eye.

"...I'm not sure about Lady Sayo. She is the kind of person who can do anything, and do it well, but I've never seen her cook before."

"Oh, okay."

If even Miss Koyuki had never seen her mother cook, then there was no hope, and Mahiru immediately gave up on the idea.

I wish I could have eaten her cooking, just once.

Her mother was always rushing around, silent and busy, and Mahiru hardly ever even saw her.

The first time Mahiru had heard that, in most normal families, one of the parents fixed the meals, she hadn't been able to hide her surprise.

It had also taken a little time for her to understand that not every household had a housekeeper, once she was old enough to question it.

"Young lady, would you prefer a meal that Lady Sayo made?"

At Miss Koyuki's question, Mahiru shook her head from side to side.

"My mother almost never comes home... I would hate to bother her."

Mahiru could count on her fingers the number of times she had seen her mother.

She saw her only about once or twice a year, and even when she did, her mother just did something else in the house and then left again without even looking at Mahiru.

Her father seemed to be even busier with work than her mother was, and when he did come home, he avoided looking at her and then left not long after.

As long as Mahiru had been aware, Miss Koyuki had been looking after all of her needs, and it seemed as if everything had been arranged for her, because she never wanted for anything.

The only thing that troubled her was a growing feeling of loneliness.

Even though she had said she wanted to eat her mother's cooking, Mahiru, who had been abandoned by her parents, knew that wish would never come true, and she was afraid of being rejected, so she had never even asked.

Sending her hair swaying loosely around her face, Mahiru shook her head, and Miss Koyuki frowned sadly. She looked troubled.

"Um, I like your cooking, Miss Koyuki. It's delicious every day, and it makes me happy. So it's okay."

Mahiru didn't want to make Miss Koyuki sad, so she hurriedly shook her head and put on a smile, but Miss Koyuki's expression darkened even more, and Mahiru didn't know what she should do.

But soon that expression vanished, and Miss Koyuki was wearing her usual smile again.

Mahiru was startled by the change and couldn't tell what Miss Koyuki was thinking anymore.

The only thing she did know was that Miss Koyuki had put on a soft smile to try to reassure her.

"Thank you very much. Just hearing you say that makes me happy, young lady."

"Um, it wasn't flattery. Your cooking really is good."

"Yes, I know that. You always seem to really enjoy it."

"Oh, good."

From the bottom of her heart, Mahiru thought everything Miss Koyuki made was delicious, so she didn't want to be mistaken for a liar.

Mahiru felt relieved Miss Koyuki had gone back to wearing the same smiling face she always wore. She watched as Miss Koyuki packed away the leftovers from dinner.

Miss Koyuki always put the dinner leftovers in plastic containers so Mahiru could eat them the following morning. While Miss Koyuki couldn't come start her housework early in the day, Miss Koyuki could still provide Mahiru with breakfast.

Thanks to this, Mahiru never missed a meal, but she still found it lonely to eat breakfast by herself every morning.

"I've got an idea. How would you like to cook with me next time, young lady?"

As she finished preparing for the next morning, Miss Koyuki saw Mahiru was staring intently at the food, and she gently broached the subject.

Because they were generally dangerous, Mahiru had been strictly ordered never to approach any heating elements, so Miss Koyuki's proposal took her completely by surprise. Her big round eyes got even rounder, and she looked up at her caregiver.

"I could do that?"

"Yes. If you can promise you'll only do it while I'm here and watching you."

"I—I promise!"

That was an easy enough promise to make.

If she broke her promise, Miss Koyuki would get angry and might leave, so Mahiru had no intention of breaking her promise. Besides, she had a feeling it would be delightful to learn from Miss Koyuki and not so pleasant to do on her own.

"Excellent. If you learn how to cook, young lady, you will have fewer troubles in the future."

"Troubles…?"

"Well, just for example, when you grow up and you live on your own."

"I'm alone now, though?"

"…When you're an adult and live by your own means, that is. If you can't cook, young lady, what will you do about meals?"

"…I'll get hungry."

"That's right. You will get hungry, won't you? So what will you do?"

"Mmm…buy something…?"

If she couldn't cook for herself, then the only way she could think of to have a meal was to eat at a restaurant, or to buy the food and take it home, or employ someone like Miss Koyuki.

"Ordering in is fine, but it might be no one is selling your favorite dishes. When you want to eat your favorite foods, what will you do?"

"…I'll have to…make them?"

"That's right. Young lady, you have lots of favorite foods, don't you? If you learn to make them yourself, every day will be enjoyable, don't you think?"

"I do think so!"

At the time, Mahiru wasn't able to imagine herself skillfully cooking her meals, but she was also confident that if Miss Koyuki would teach her, she could probably learn.

She was sure she would be happy if she learned to make all sorts of different foods, like Miss Koyuki could.

Every day Mahiru had all sorts of foods prepared for her, and she really enjoyed her meals, so she was sure it would be even better if she could make the food herself.

Mahiru did honestly think that, and when she gave Miss Koyuki her cheerful answer, Miss Koyuki must also have been relieved, because she put on a gentle smile.

"I'm so glad to hear you're also interested in cooking, young lady. I will teach you to make anything that I'm able to."

"Like fluffy omurice?"

"Yes, omurice, beef stew, miso soup, the stew you had today—you'll learn to make all of them."

"Really, I will?"

"Yes."

When she heard she would learn to make the dishes that had been produced by Miss Koyuki's magic hands, Mahiru's heart leapt in her chest.

"Will I also learn to make my father and mother's favorite foods?"

Maybe if she was learning to make all sorts of different dishes…

She wondered if her parents, who currently never so much as glanced her way, might finally look at her.

She wondered if they might even eat a meal together.

Full of such hopes but unable to voice them, she had asked Miss

Koyuki her question. Miss Koyuki cast her eyes downward slightly but patted Mahiru's head with the same smile on her face.

Normally, Miss Koyuki hardly touched her, and Mahiru narrowed her eyes and fully savored the pleasant feeling of Miss Koyuki's palm running gently over her hair.

"That's a good question. I think you'll learn to make them someday."

"Then I'll work really hard!"

Mahiru put as much energy and enthusiasm as she could into her answer.

"It's late now, so you mustn't shout," chided Miss Koyuki.

But Mahiru grinned broadly and embraced the fleeting hope that if she tried her hardest, she might earn the attention of her parents. She was looking forward to her cooking lessons.

Well, the story doesn't have a particularly happy ending, though.

Gazing down at the page filled with scratchy, childish letters, Mahiru let out a very quiet little sigh, so that Amane, sitting beside her, wouldn't notice.

It seemed like the most obvious thing in the world now, but even after Mahiru learned how to cook, her parents never paid her any mind.

Rather, even when they had the opportunity to have some slight contact with her, they never showed any interest in asking about it, and she didn't volunteer to tell them, either.

Miss Koyuki had probably kept them informed, so if they had read through her reports properly, they must have at least known that she had learned how to cook.

Looking back on things now, Mahiru understood the truth that they must have at least skimmed the letters, but she also knew they never offered any acknowledgment to their young daughter, who was putting in lots of effort, and that was the harsh reality.

The shaky words in her diary, blurred by once wet pages, eloquently conveyed the feelings she'd had at that time better than anything else could.

…I was young, and foolish.

At the time, she had thought if she worked hard, she might get them to pay a little attention to her.

From the perspective of present-day Mahiru, who knew about her parents' attitude and stance toward her, she could declare that the person who had held such hopes was a fool, but she understood perfectly well it would have been impossible for the child Mahiru to have predicted that.

As a result, she'd been betrayed by her own naive hopes and had entered her feelings into her diary, crying into it as she wrote. She didn't enjoy looking through these entries.

I got my hopes up all on my own and got my feelings hurt, I made myself cry and suffer all by myself.

Miss Koyuki hadn't lied to her.

She had said she was sure Mahiru would learn to make the dishes but had never said a word about being able to get her parents to eat them.

Miss Koyuki must have made the expression she did precisely because even she could tell Mahiru's wish was never going to come true.

Miss Koyuki had probably thought that if she'd asked Mahiru's parents, they would have said something cruel, but Mahiru was still grateful to her.

At that time, Miss Koyuki had known her parents but had been nothing more than their employee, and that had probably been all she could say about it.

There was no way she could break the heart of someone so young, who still wanted to cling to her mama and papa.

Even though she had known the truth, Miss Koyuki must have

figured it would be less damaging if Mahiru learned it after she was grown.

Thanks to Miss Koyuki's lessons, Mahiru could cook almost anything. She had developed her skills and could easily prepare dishes she'd never made before, just by looking at a recipe.

And that wasn't all. Miss Koyuki had trained Mahiru in all facets of life, probably out of the kindness of her heart, so Mahiru would be able to live on her own in the future.

Miss Koyuki had her own home.

To put it simply, she was, in the end, an outsider, and she wasn't going to be with Mahiru forever. Mahiru was not Miss Koyuki's child; she was a child Miss Koyuki was looking after as a job.

It was exactly because she knew they would part ways someday that she had taught Mahiru things from such a young age, so Mahiru would not struggle later.

She had been much more of a parent to Mahiru than Mahiru's own parents, Mahiru now knew.

…I'm truly grateful.

Thanks to Miss Koyuki, Mahiru had acquired the skills to live on her own.

And she had found someone who meant more to her than anyone else.

"I'm sure your cooking will help you find someone who'll make you happy, Mahiru."

Mahiru recalled the kind and sincere words Miss Koyuki had said to her the one and only time when she stepped out of her role as hired help and dropped her formal way of speaking.

I found him, Miss Koyuki.

Mahiru had found someone who only had eyes for her, who loved only her, someone who treasured her and wanted to build a happy life with her.

As she mused that someday she'd like to go see Miss Koyuki in person and introduce her to Amane, Mahiru traced the tip of her finger over the anguished words her younger self had left behind.

"Someday in the future, someone precious will come into your life, someone who only has eyes for you."

Holding back tears as she remembered her younger self confiding in her diary, Mahiru silently encouraged that girl not to give up.

Cute Kids

"Really, I don't know what to do about this."

It was quite late at night, late enough that the kids were each resting in their own rooms, one in his bedroom and one in the guest room.

Shihoko had apparently had a little bit of work left to finish at home. She'd come down into the living room, grumbling and sighing in frustration. Shuuto thought carefully about what might be bothering his wife.

"Something about work?" he asked. "Are they being unreasonable about your deadlines?"

"Ah, no, no, I'm talking about the thing earlier, with Amane."

When he heard her mention the thing with Amane, Shuuto immediately knew what was troubling Shihoko.

"The thing with the Toujou boy?"

"Yeah. It sounds like he was bugging him again. You know, ever since they started high school, it's like he's gone wild or something. I've been hearing about it from the other wives I know, and it sounds like he's turned into kind of a rascal."

Just recently, when Amane and his guest had gone for a

walk, they'd had the misfortune of running into the other boy as soon as they'd stepped outside. They'd heard as much from Amane himself.

It sounded like it had really been a chance reunion. It was impossible to imagine Amane had deliberately gone to see him. Though it might be conceivable Toujou, having heard Amane was coming home, had planned to run into him.

"Well, as long as Amane's gotten over it, I don't think we should say anything. Especially since it doesn't seem like the Toujou boy did anything to him. If he had, I'm sure we'd see it in the way both Amane and Miss Shiina were behaving."

Without peering into their hearts, Amane's parents couldn't know exactly what had happened, but at least they didn't see any signs Amane had been hurt. In other words, his contact with Toujou had affected Amane only mildly.

And given what they knew about Mahiru's personality, if Amane was suffering, she would probably be wearing a sorrowful expression, and she would likely find a way to casually report what had happened to Shihoko, so Shihoko was fairly certain nothing much had happened.

And his wounds have all completely healed, too.

It was all deeply emotional for Shuuto, who knew how low Amane's spirits had once sunk.

Amane had been used and betrayed. Then later, the same boys who had hurt him had turned Amane's classmates against him, which had hurt him badly at the time.

Shuuto regretted that neither he nor Shihoko had noticed what was going on with Toujou, or had reprimanded him for his behavior toward others.

Before all that happened, they had showered Amane with affection and made sure he wanted for nothing. Thanks to that, Amane had grown into a sincere child, who was honest and never distrusted anyone, which had been his downfall.

Only after his son was broken did Shuuto realize someone raised in perfect conditions was easier to break than someone who'd had experienced just the right amount of hardship.

Well, in the end, he grew into a fine young man, but still…

Everything that had happened, and all the hurt it had caused, had shaped the person Amane became, so it hadn't been entirely bad. At least that's how it seemed to them now, in hindsight. At the time, they had been beside themselves with worry.

"That's true, but…as his mother, I still worry, you know?"

Shihoko always worried the most about their son, even though she teased him. Shuuto patted her head, and after glancing down the hallway, he smiled at his wife.

"If he's been able to overcome it on his own and change the way he thinks about his past, then I don't have anything in particular to say about it."

"You're very calm about this, Shuuto."

"I don't know if I'm calm exactly, but I trust him, our Amane."

"Whereas I can't help but feel like Mama needs to step in and do something, when I see my darling only son sniffling and sobbing!"

"Amane would object to that if he heard you. He'd say, 'I'm not crying!' And I also don't think you'd be the one he'd turn to for help, Shihoko."

"Well, I suppose if he was crying, he'd get comfort from sweet Mahiru, so he probably doesn't need his old mother anymore, *sniff.*"

"Was that a sniffle I heard?"

"Stop picking at little details."

Shihoko was cutely pretending to cry, but Shuuto could tell she was genuinely concerned, so he comforted her, stroking her head intermittently.

However, she must have had more to say about the incident with Toujou, because even though Shuuto comforted her, he could see she was still slightly on edge.

"Even so, the Toujous must be having a hard time of it, too. He must be making life difficult for his parents."

"He sure is. Now, it wasn't our obligation to say anything, but we were a little late in confronting the issue. It sounds like he really got out of control after the boys started middle school, you know."

What they'd realized when they looked into things after the incident with Amane was that Toujou had started hanging out with those kinds of friends after entering middle school and that his new companions had rapidly tipped the scales.

It was around this time they picked up on what the boy's home environment was like.

Shihoko had always claimed Toujou's parents were good people, but from where Shuuto stood, that assessment didn't seem quite right.

Sure, Toujou's parents were sociable and had pleasant personalities. And he also knew they were a polite, honest, and kind couple.

However, what Shuuto sensed was that this was only what they showed to other people.

When he looked at their boy, it was easy to tell their efforts to be pure and righteous had gone off track, and that had manifested in their son.

Shihoko and Shuuto themselves had also warped Amane in certain ways, or rather, they'd caused him problems by failing to teach him that his innocence could make him an unwitting target for the darkness in the world. But a different kind of difficulty in childrearing had become apparent in the Toujou household.

"The rebellious years are a difficult time. I was actually worried because Amane didn't rebel very much."

"Amane had a little bit of a rebellious phase, but that was the least of our worries then, wasn't it?"

"The timing was just awful. To have something like that happen at such a sensitive stage…"

"It was actually concerning because he was too good of a kid, I remember. Even though I was looking forward to getting yelled at, and called 'stupid old man!'"

Shuuto had been prepared for that kind of a rebellious phase, but Amane was a well-behaved child to begin with, so he hadn't pushed back against his parents all that much, and in fact, he had grown into a tenderhearted young man, which was somewhat anticlimactic.

"I wonder what it says about you, that you were looking forward to something like that?"

"I mean, I was like that, so I thought I'd be able to take it in stride when he called me names, like it's just part of growing up."

"…Your father did say you didn't really settle down until you were almost out of high school or just starting college, Shuuto."

"Ah-ha-ha. But you know, it wasn't the sort of thing that hurt anyone else. I just did stupid stuff with my friends. I would classify it as not knowing how to behave; that's all."

His response came out sounding a little like a dig at the person who had brought up the topic a moment ago, but that wasn't intentional.

Even so, it seemed like it had dredged up memories for her. When Shihoko sighed softly, Shuuto knew he had messed up, and he felt a little remorseful.

"The Toujou boy still hasn't changed at all, has he?"

"Sounds that way. Compared to Amane and his friends, he seems to be the same as he was years ago. Amane, on the other hand, has changed so much, it's startling."

"Oh, he really has changed, our Amane."

Both Shuuto and Shihoko nodded in unison whenever anyone asked if Amane was different now.

When they'd sent Amane out on his own, confident he would overcome his hurt feelings, he had been totally introverted, misanthropic, and brusque, and he'd had a cold way of talking that didn't allow people to get close to him. But the Amane who had come home to visit had completely transformed.

He had this tenderness and composure that would have been unbelievable half a year earlier, and the confidence exuding from him now lit up his whole expression.

His parents had been quite concerned about him for a while, but Amane's wounds had healed, and he had grown into such an upright young man they verifiably didn't need to worry any longer.

"It's a relief to see he's changed in a positive direction. I wasn't sure how things would turn out when he left home, but letting him go was the right thing to do, wasn't it?"

"You're right. There are parts of a child that can't develop under the loving protection of his parents, so it's gratifying to see he's done some growing up since leaving."

"Heh-heh, and the trigger for that growth was definitely the idea of someone like dear Mahiru becoming a member of the Fujimiya family, don't you think?"

"Love can push someone to mature very quickly."

"People never do change, do they, without something to kick-start it?"

There were very few people who could make up their own minds to change without any kind of push. Most people first started to change when something or other gave them a push on the back to get them going.

In Amane's case, that had been Mahiru; that was all.

"I'm glad Amane got over all of that so quickly, but…I worry that boy might get fixated on Amane. I mean, people hold on to grudges sometimes, right?"

"The fact there's physical distance between them sets my mind at ease. And anyway, the Toujou boy may be on the wrong path, but I think he has enough sense not to do anything truly terrible. I don't think he has the nerve to cross any hard lines. For better or worse, I think he's really just a kid who's easily scared trying to seem tougher than he is."

"You're strangely confident, considering how bitter you are about the whole thing."

"I looked into him a little bit, and that's the conclusion I came to after looking at his present situation."

"…You work fast."

Shihoko gave him an astonished look, and Shuuto smiled back at her.

He had investigated Toujou's circumstances at the time, too, and had recently been checking again to a certain degree, wondering what was driving his present-day behavior and attitude.

He had looked into everything he could, from his previous home environment to his current home environment, from his parents' working environments to his school environment, and made his judgment based on that.

Sure enough, Toujou's character hadn't changed, and he seemed to be behaving in high school just as he had been in middle school, stubbornly refusing to develop beyond being a mischievous kid.

He seemed to be venting his frustration on a daily basis while staying just out of the reach of the law, so he hadn't gone so far as to cross the last lines of decency his parents had drilled into him. At least, as far as Shuuto could see, that was how it seemed.

"There's no way I wouldn't look into someone who might do harm to my son. I'll make use of any means I can. I have acquaintances among his current teachers and neighbors, so I enlisted their help."

"Maybe you work a little too quickly?"

"The faster I work, the faster we can see what our options are, right?"

Rather than always being one step behind, they ought to make the first move. It would be too late if he had waited to investigate until after something had already happened. If it was possible to prevent something from happening ahead of time, surely that was the better option.

"He was going through a major rebellious phase and that might've been the end of it, but when his parents tried to rein him in, he had a major outburst instead. That's all for now, but…"

Though he was hostile toward his parents and seemed depressed, the boy wasn't really a bad kid.

That more or less described his present situation.

"Well, in any case…Amane probably doesn't intend to come back here again, even after he graduates. He plans to attend college over there, too. And I haven't told the people around here what high school Amane is attending. How about you, Shihoko? You've only said he went to a different prefecture, right?"

"Yes. Just in case."

"Once he graduates from college and starts working, it will be even harder for anyone to track him down. And I doubt the Toujou boy has the tenacity to chase him that far."

Shuuto was on alert just in case he did hit rock bottom, but he was just barely staying on solid footing for the time being. And Toujou had to know even if he did fixate on Amane, nothing would come of it.

Because he was no longer a part of Amane's world.

"Besides..."

"Besides?"

"There won't be a next time."

If, on the very off chance, he tried to do some kind of harm to Amane again, Shuuto would justifiably take suitable action.

He had forgiven the first offense. He wouldn't forgive a second.

No matter what kind of background the boy had, no matter what his motives, the Fujimiyas had no margin for taking extenuating circumstances into consideration.

As the victims, they had no interest in the motivations of the aggressor. If he tried to hurt Amane again, they would have no choice but to make sure he couldn't do any further damage to them, and that was all there was to it.

They would get him to understand firsthand what he had done and what he was trying to do, and they would take measures to ensure he never appeared before Amane ever again.

"...I think you're the one who's angriest about it, Shuuto."

"I am angry. Or rather, I feel justified in getting rid of him if he becomes an obstacle for Amane, I suppose."

If there was a bug trying to devour a tree trunk that was growing tall and beautiful, it would only be natural to deal with it. At least until the tree was finished growing, until it had developed its own defenses and could deal with the bug itself, it was proper for caretakers to look after it.

Even if a child eventually set down roots and built a home somewhere far away, it was in a parent's nature to want to protect them while they were still a child under their parents' guardianship.

"Doesn't that count as being angry?"

"Mmm...I'm not angry. But I also haven't forgiven him."

Shuuto was not holding on to his anger toward Toujou. It was a waste of energy and mental space, and as long as he wasn't doing anything, Shuuto wouldn't consider making any moves on his end.

However, he still remembered what the boy had done, and he wasn't willing to simply forgive and forget. That was all.

"Shuuto, you sure can hold a grudge."

"Well, now. I'm sure everyone experiences frustrations in this life, but if someone tries to stab you in the back, you have to act accordingly."

"I was so scared back then. From the time you started using your personal connections and actively investigating the family, I believed you were seriously angry, you know."

"Parents protect their children, after all. And because you gave me a lot of emotional support, Shihoko, I was able to work behind the scenes. I couldn't have done it without you."

"...You didn't do anything, though, did you?"

"No, I didn't. That was his first offense, so I let him get off with a warning."

"What about the second time?"

"I'm no saint. And I see no reason to wait for a third time."

It was ridiculous to think he would forgive violence twice. Of course, he would make an effort to ensure it didn't happen, but if it did happen a second time, the moment that it did, he had every intention of eliminating the threat.

"Now, if it stays in the realm of a quarrel between two children, then as a parent, I won't do anything, but if it goes beyond that, then it falls into the domain of the adults. Before my child gets mixed up in something that hurts him, it's my job as a grown-up to take care of it."

If bullying progressed to defamation, threats, and acts of violence, there was no longer anything that a child could do.

That was the point where adult intervention was necessary, and the perpetrator should be punished in accordance with the law.

There was probably no longer any need to worry about that for Amane, but the best thing to do was to be prepared, Shuuto concluded, and he leaned back against the sofa.

Shihoko wore a contemplative look on her face but ultimately agreed with him and let out a little sigh. That was the moment the living room door let in a little fresh air from the hallway.

The sound of the hinges squeaking cut through the quiet night.

When they both looked in that direction, the door was slightly ajar, and Mahiru was peeking in at them, looking uncomfortable.

"Oh, Mahiru dear, what's the matter? What are you doing up this late?"

In an instant, Shihoko's expression brightened, and she put on a smile. Hesitantly, with a worried look on her face, Mahiru stepped into the living room.

It didn't sound like Mahiru was usually awake at this hour, so apparently she had either woken up again or hadn't been able to go to sleep.

"Ah, well, um…I thought I might be able to get some water…"

"Oh, water? Wait just a moment, okay? You can have a seat right there."

"Oh, no, sorry to bother you."

"It's fine, it's fine. Make yourself at home."

Shihoko was suddenly in much higher spirits. She got up and trotted toward the kitchen, keeping her footsteps quiet, and her husband, Shuuto, couldn't help but smile at how quickly she had changed gears.

He shouldn't have been surprised that Mahiru, who was in someone else's home, didn't seem able to shake her reserve. In a truly timid manner, she walked over to him and bobbed her head in a little bow.

"Um, I'm sorry for intruding."

"Oh, no, we don't mind. You don't need to be so formal or apologize for anything."

©Hanekoto

"Right, right, we're all living under one roof here!" Shihoko said.

"You're right, we're all living here, if only for a limited time."

"Oh now, Shuuto, don't throw cold water on my dreams! I'm the only one who needs to pour water right now."

When Shuuto cut in, thinking that from Mahiru's perspective, it would be preferable just to add Amane first, rather than suddenly gaining a whole family living under one roof together, he heard Shihoko's huffy voice come back from the kitchen, along with the sound of water being poured from the mouth of a plastic bottle.

After a little while, Shihoko came back holding a tray with three glasses on it, and she handed one of them to Mahiru with a broad smile.

"Here, go ahead."

"Thank you very much."

"You have some, too, Shuuto. You must be thirsty."

"I guess I am."

That night they had talked a lot more than usual. When Shuuto looked at the clock, he saw that an hour had gone by without them noticing it. It was always like that when they got absorbed in conversation, and he had been the biggest talker this time. He smiled wryly at the thought.

When he brought his glass to his mouth, he realized he must have gotten heated without knowing it. The water felt extremely cold going down his throat.

He mused that he could still be immature sometimes, and he reflected on how recklessly he was ready to behave for the sake of his dear son as he quietly attempted to cool down. For some reason, Mahiru was looking at him with her eyes narrowed a little bit.

Shihoko also seemed to be thirsty from talking, and she enthusiastically drained her glass and set it on the table. She watched as Mahiru slowly finished drinking her water, then she smiled at the girl.

"By the way, don't tell Amane what we were just talking about, okay?"

"Ah—"

Though he suspected she had overheard them, Shuuto was wavering over whether or not to say anything when Shihoko readily came out and said it. Mahiru suddenly went pale.

But Shihoko seemed to understand what she'd said could sound like she was criticizing Mahiru, and she immediately waved her hand back and forth in a panic and insisted that wasn't the case.

"Ah, I don't mean to blame you for overhearing, okay?! It's our fault for talking so long and loudly enough for our voices to make it out into the hallway!"

Mahiru was wearing an expression of unconcealed guilt for eavesdropping on their conversation, so Shihoko's concern was understandable.

"Ohhh, I'm sorry, honey. I didn't mean to make you feel bad. You don't need to worry about it, okay?"

"Shihoko, you should have simply said you'd be embarrassed to let Amane hear what we were saying and asked her not to mention it."

"N-nothing to be done now."

As things stood, they were in danger of misunderstanding each other, so Shuuto offered Shihoko a lifeboat, and she flushed slightly and raised her eyebrows in a troubled expression.

"If we worry over him too much, I'm sure he'll tell us not to treat him like a child, and that he's doing fine now, you know? In truth, when I see how Amane's doing, it's obvious that he's just fine, but I'm his mother, so I still worry, of course. Even though he's already a splendid young man, in our minds he's still our darling little boy."

Shuuto also understood Shihoko's feelings very well, and his own sentiments were similar enough to get him all worked up just a few moments earlier, so Shuuto smiled as he listened to Shihoko talk. But when Mahiru had suddenly crumpled her face up in distress, both Shihoko and Shuuto panicked.

Mahiru's face fell in a much sadder expression than earlier when she had mistakenly thought she was being criticized, and she looked like she might cry at any moment. Her caramel-colored eyes were nearly overflowing with big wet teardrops about to fall from them.

And yet not a single drop spilled over, and she just sat there pressing her lips tightly together, looking like she was on the verge of tears.

"By any chance did I say something to hurt your feelings, sweetie?"

"N-not at all. It's just…I was just thinking how nice it must be."

They knew right away what she was talking about.

They had heard about Mahiru's situation to a certain degree and about what kind of environment she'd grown up in.

Amane's parents and Mahiru's parents were different enough that it wouldn't be a stretch to call them polar opposites. Her parents had been unbelievably indifferent to her and had, in fact, abandoned most of their duties as parents.

It must have been painful for Mahiru, who had basically never been treated like a child by her own parents, to see Shuuto and Shihoko treasure Amane so.

A silent scream was seeping out from her body, demanding to know why things hadn't been that way for her, and the overwhelming sorrow of it made Shuuto frown.

…*Parents who would let their own daughter make a face like this are no parents at all.*

Parents were human, too.

They had likes and dislikes, got along with some people and didn't get along with others, and had their own circumstances to contend with. He couldn't insist every parent had to love and prioritize their child unconditionally.

He didn't mean to condemn them for being unable to love her.

That wasn't something that an outsider could judge lightly.

But what he did think was—

Even if they couldn't love her, given that they brought her into this world, they had a moral responsibility toward her.

And that the kind of people who would abandon the work of parenting and make their child cry, despite having decided to become parents in the first place, simply should not exist.

Though Mahiru's parents were strangers to him, he resented them tremendously, and behind his calm expression, Shuuto was suppressing the anger that welled up inside him. He gazed quietly at Mahiru, who sat silently, looking younger than usual, like a little lost child braving her sadness.

"...You don't need to envy Amane, you know? After all, as far as we are concerned, you're already like a daughter to us, Mahiru dear."

Shihoko said exactly what Shuuto had been thinking, and he smiled, feeling relieved they felt the same way.

"Huh?" Mahiru must not have been expecting that. It seemed to put her at a loss for words.

"Oh no, maybe that was too hasty. Did I jump to the wrong conclusion?"

"Ah, n-no, that is…you didn't…um…?"

"Oh my."

"Shihoko, don't tease the girl. But I also think of you just like a daughter, you know."

When he agreed with what his wife had said, the sadness faded from Mahiru's expression, which was then filled with confusion.

Shuuto continued, to make doubly sure she understood, and Mahiru listened, frozen solid.

"To begin with, you're someone who our Amane, who was a late bloomer and who essentially never trusted anyone, has come to love and trust deeply. We trust you, too, and from the time we've spent with you so far, we know quite well you are a good girl, Miss Shiina."

"…A good girl… I'm not really… I just seem that way."

"Your definition of being a good girl is different from what we're thinking of, Mahiru sweetheart."

Mahiru's body had jumped in reaction to the words *good girl*, so Shihoko gave her a smile that was packed with plenty of cheer and affection.

"When we say you're a good girl, we mean that you're head over heels for Amane and you love-love-love him."

"Ah, um…"

"Come on, Shihoko. There had to be a better way of saying things." He chided Shihoko.

But Shihoko showed zero intent to retract her statement. "I think that was perfectly easy to understand," she said.

Worried that Mahiru might misunderstand if they left it at that, Shuuto maintained his gentle smile as he continued talking to Mahiru, whose cheeks had turned red out of embarrassment.

"…Miss Shiina, you've come to care for our son a lot, haven't you? We know you have earnest feelings for him and you want to make a happy life with him. You're not seeking happiness just for yourself, or just for Amane, but to make a happy life together, we can tell."

It was perfectly obvious from a parent's perspective that Mahiru loved Amane from the bottom of her heart and that Amane was also in love with her.

They could sense the two of them cared for each other and respected each other, they could feel their determination to make a life together, and they were relieved to hear they were, in fact, already basically living together in the city.

They figured that, with these two kids, that was just fine.

"We've seen that even when something difficult happens, the two of you will work together to overcome it. You're a girl I could trust with Amane…which is a strange way of putting it maybe. We think you're just wonderful, and we want to see your relationship develop."

"Actually, I worry a little bit about leaving things up to Amane, so Mahiru dear, you can go ahead and take the initiative anytime."

"Hey now, Amane's grown a lot!"

"I know that, but…"

With a grimace, Shuuto chided Shihoko, who tended to show favoritism to Mahiru at times like these. At the same time, he gave Mahiru, who was wearing an expression full of surprise, a gentle look.

"We've already accepted you for who you are, Miss Shiina. We think of you like family, and we'd like to help you if you ever have any trouble."

No matter what happened, Shihoko and Shuuto could never become Mahiru's real parents.

Even so, as adults who had a connection to her, they could offer her a helping hand. They could scoop her up and rescue her if she fell into the darkness.

"If at any time things with your family become too difficult, you come to us. We can be your shelter, and there are methods for getting you out of their family register, for example, as an adopted child to us or to a relative of ours."

"The extreme option is that you could marry into the family without a guardian's permission, after you become an adult. Hurry up and become an adult already, would you?"

Shuuto patted Shihoko's head lightly for being so impatient and tried to put the brakes on her delusions.

However, he had a feeling that, in this case, it wasn't a delusion and that it might very well become reality.

That was how strong the relationship of mutual trust between Amane and Mahiru was. They seemed quite determined and ready for the future, more so than he and Shihoko had once been when they'd started dating.

The Fujimiya family was made up entirely of single-minded, earnest people.

In all likelihood, so long as Mahiru didn't object, Amane was not going to change his plans.

She would probably end up taking the Fujimiya name sooner or later. Shuuto wondered if that might allow her to say farewell to all of her painful memories.

"Mahiru sweetie, you're still a child for a while longer, so if things get tough, you can rely on dependable adults. If you have problems, you should confide in us. If you think we can help, we'll do all that we can to support you."

Shihoko stared straight at her as she said this, and she squeezed Mahiru's trembling hand. Mahiru was hanging her head as she gave a small nod.

Shuuto pretended like he didn't see the teardrop fall on the arm Shihoko had wrapped around the girl.

After a little while, Mahiru raised her head, and though the area around her eyes was slightly red, her expression had become much more cheerful.

When she smiled at Shihoko, who had silently held her hand the whole time, she no longer had the look of a little lost child.

"In exchange for not telling Amane about your conversation earlier, I'd ask that you also not tell him that I almost cried, please."

"Sure, it's a promise. If one of us breaks it…let's see… How about they get punished with a hug?"

"Heh-heh, that's not a punishment!"

"Oh, Shuuto, did you hear that? I wish Amane would learn from her; the boy's really stopped being cute these days."

Even though she herself had proposed it as a punishment, Shihoko took it upon herself to throw her arms around Mahiru, hugging her anyway, and Mahiru happily accepted it.

A delighted smile rose to Shuuto's lips as he watched Mahiru, who welcomed the so-called punishment with open arms.

"Oh, you're so cute! Since we don't get many opportunities like this, will you come sleep in my room?" Shihoko asked excitedly. "We can stay up talking about boys!"

"If you do that, I won't have anywhere to sleep," Shuuto pointed out.

"What if you go sleep with Amane?"

"I'd rather not; that seems like it'd cause some screaming in the morning. It's not right to go sneaking into someone's bedroom, and I'm sure at his age, Amane would rather not share a bed with his father."

It was obvious to him doing that would result in Amane giving him the silent treatment, so he slowly shook his head with an awkward smile.

There must have been something funny about their exchange, because Mahiru let a little laugh out, prompting Shuuto and Shihoko to look at each other with a grin.

Unwanted Contact

Really, why is this happening now?

Ever since Mahiru had heard about Amane's encounter with her father, Asahi, and their conversation, that question had been swirling around in her mind, obstructing her thoughts.

To Mahiru, the creatures known as parents were like a sort of apparition—she didn't see them as being truly solid.

She recognized them as the genetic donors who had created her, but she had absolutely no conception of them as the people who had raised her. Ever since she had been aware of things, the person who had taught Mahiru how to live, along with just about everything else, was the woman who was her housekeeper as well as her private tutor, Miss Koyuki. Not her parents.

Even so, when she was young, she had wanted her parents to notice her, so she'd worked hard and approached them, but they hadn't reciprocated.

They had unambiguously rejected her.

All they had done was give birth to her, then leave her on her own without even taking care of her, to prioritize the things they themselves wanted to do.

That was Mahiru's experience with parents.

At the very beginning, she had wanted them to look at her, wanted them to love her, and she had desperately reached out for them, but there was no way they could know the despair she had felt on the day when she realized it was all futile. They didn't have the first clue about how badly that had hurt her, and they had probably never even considered it.

They also didn't know about how, ever since then, Mahiru had been living with this terrible disappointment in her parents, while still holding on to a minuscule feeling of hope. She no longer cared if they knew.

Though she had mostly given up on being loved, she clung to the possibility they might pay her some—any—attention like someone panning for the tiniest speck of gold in an enormous river. She'd known her hope was foolish, and yet she hadn't been able to give up on it entirely, and she found it all a bit ridiculous.

With Amane around, finally she had made it to the verge of no longer craving affection from her parents.

"What does he want at this point?"

The voice that came out of her mouth was intensely cold.

Such an icy tone was almost impossible to imagine coming from Mahiru, given the angelic voice she used toward the majority of people and the normal voice she used with Amane.

But to Mahiru, the individual who happened to be her father was no longer part of her inner circle or indeed a part of her world at all. He was simply a stranger.

Mahiru didn't know, and she didn't want to know, what the person who had left all of his responsibilities up to Miss Koyuki and abandoned her without trying to make contact for over ten years was thinking or what he sought by making contact with her now.

He can't expect me to treat him like a parent now.

It would be impossible for her to view him as a father when he had never done anything for her.

As meager as it was, the one paltry defense Asahi had going for him was that he had never said anything abusive to Mahiru. In comparison to Sayo, he could be credited with that, at least. But when it came to ignoring Mahiru and everything she went through, he had been far more wicked than Sayo.

Her father, Asahi, had never done anything no matter how Mahiru suffered, and he had ultimately just averted his eyes from anything inconvenient for him and immersed himself in his work, erasing Mahiru's very existence from his mind. Her mother, Sayo, had shunned and rejected her, but she had at least recognized her daughter existed.

When she thought about which one of them had actually been worse, Mahiru found she wasn't really sure.

The only thing she knew for certain was that she had no intention of trusting or accepting Asahi, who had appeared after all this time calling himself her father and scheming to make contact with her.

I wonder what's gotten into him.

It was only natural for her to be on her guard, in case he was trying to exercise some kind of parental authority at this late stage.

According to Amane, who'd actually spoken with him, he didn't intend to cause her any harm, but supposing that were true, she didn't know what he was after, so of course she was on guard.

Perhaps Asahi himself had some appreciation of that, and that was why he hadn't tried to contact Mahiru suddenly.

As far as Mahiru was concerned, that gave her an even worse image of him, and it made her feel creeped out that he had hidden himself nearby and covertly investigated her life.

Fortunately, what she had picked up so far about Asahi's personality led her to presume he was not the controlling, tyrannical type, and he probably preferred not to rock the boat. Because of that, she reasoned that he wasn't going to try to do anything to her.

On the off chance Asahi did do something, if he tried to cause some kind of problem, Mahiru always had her diary that held a record of everything that had ever happened to her, plus her elementary and middle school teachers, who knew that her parents had almost nothing to do with her, as well as the testimony of Miss Koyuki, who had always been closest to her. If push came to shove, she would consider taking refuge in a children's welfare center.

She had told Amane her diary contained all the memories she had ever put down on paper, and while that wasn't wrong, her other purpose for writing it all down was to serve as evidence that closely documented everything that had been done to her and her feelings about it.

She wasn't clear on whether what had happened to her so far constituted child neglect, but she expected that if her father's business associates found out he was under legal scrutiny, it would affect his standing at the company. In order to protect herself, in order to protect her lifestyle, she had to be ready to retaliate however she could.

I hope it doesn't come to that, but...

Mahiru didn't want this to turn into a major incident. She wanted to keep living the way she was now, keeping her distance and having no contact with her parents.

She wanted to know the intentions of her father, who had suddenly thrown her this curveball, but if having contact with him would destroy her current lifestyle, then she would rather not know.

After all, Mahiru no longer needed her parents' love.

On a pragmatic level, she probably did need them financially. But she already had enough to cover college in her bank account, and since they had been transferring her a lot of money every month, as if they thought they could settle everything with money, she also had enough to cover her living expenses until she was about halfway through college. She had her bankbook, and her personal seal, and her accounts were in her own name, so they couldn't meddle in her affairs.

She had an unthinkable amount of money for a high school student, but that money was basically child support. It was akin to consolation money, intended to make up for their neglect.

To Mahiru, her parents were no longer people from whom she expected any affection. They were more like objects of fear, who might threaten her way of living.

She didn't need them anymore.

Even if they reached out to her at this point, she was no longer a child who would meekly grab on to them. She wasn't hungry for their attention.

Because Mahiru already found someone else to hold her hand.

Just like always, when Mahiru went over to Amane's place, he came out to greet her with a gentle smile.

Even after the incident with Asahi the other day, Amane's behavior hadn't changed. Actually, to put it more accurately, he seemed more magnanimous than usual, and he was being extra thoughtful while pretending not to know that there was anything wrong. But he seemed to be trying not to let it show on his face.

He wasn't treating her with kid gloves, nor was he being insensitive. He was simply being calm and balanced in how he treated her, and at the moment, Mahiru was grateful for that.

When she entered the living room at Amane's urging, chilly air greeted her.

She knew what temperature he usually had the air conditioner set to, so she was sure it shouldn't have made the room so cool, but when she snuggled up close to Amane, feeling somewhat unpleasantly cold, he smiled a little and pulled her over by the hand and sat her down on the couch.

As Mahiru sank into the cushions, and Amane took a seat beside her, she looked at him and noticed he was wearing his usual expression, but there was a tender look in his eyes.

"Amane?"

When she timidly called the name of the boy she loved, he answered her with a smile that was as gentle as summer sunshine.

Under that smile, warm enough to make snow melt, she felt the haze that had been swirling in her chest begin to dissipate.

Even so, the feelings that had bubbled up after the incident the other day didn't just disappear. Ultimately, at the center of all that haze, there was something heavy and hard, like a lump that had been condensing there. It was like she had just remembered it existed and now she constantly felt its presence.

"Yeah, what's up?" he asked her back in a voice so soft, it would have once been unimaginable coming from him. Mahiru let her eyes wander, unsure how to answer.

She hadn't really wanted Amane to do anything in particular. But she wanted to be beside him, and she scooted over to him.

"…It's, um… Hold my hand, please."

She had thought about it and had made this small request.

The only person who Mahiru wanted to hold hands with, the only one who was allowed, was Amane.

Maybe she wanted to remind herself of that again.

Though she hesitated a little when she asked, in response to her request, Amane put on a soft smile, and then took Mahiru's hand in his.

His slightly bony, somewhat clumsy, yet sturdy hands were the first ones she'd ever wanted to touch her. They were always gentle and careful.

Just feeling those hands was enough to settle her down so much, she almost felt deflated.

"Just your hand?" Amane asked gently but a little mischievously, as if to question whether she wanted to add on any other options.

Mahiru cast her eyes downward, not sure whether she could presume upon him further.

In the end, there hadn't been any further contact from Asahi. Her normal daily life had returned, as if nothing had ever happened.

Since she was just indecisively worrying over things on her own, she wasn't sure whether it was all right to lean on Amane more than she already was, and she hesitated to say anything. Amane squeezed her hand a little, and his warmth gently left her side.

She let out a little noise of protest, and in that same moment, a blanket was tossed over Mahiru's head.

"…You're chillier than usual today, huh, Mahiru? Maybe I have the air conditioner up too high. Here, wrap yourself up in this blanket," he said with a smile.

Mahiru wasn't yet completely chilled by the air conditioner, but he wrapped her body up in the blanket, put his arms around her back and under her knees, and lifted her easily, without any hesitation.

He cradled her in his arms and set her right down into his lap. Mahiru blinked in surprise and confusion. As he peered down at her, Amane's obsidian-black eyes narrowed affectionately.

"Warmer now?"

"…Yes."

Though she felt her face growing hot from the way Amane had shown he could carry her in his arms without any hesitation at all, she knew Amane had been very careful to not touch on the delicate fact that Mahiru had been struggling with all kinds of thoughts lately, so Mahiru smiled to make sure the heat in her cheeks didn't leak out from the corners of her eyes.

He probably thought her smile was a bluff, but she didn't mind him thinking that. She was confident Amane would accept her even so.

Though she heard a very slightly strained sigh from above, Mahiru didn't look up at Amane's expression; she simply pressed her cheek into his chest, which had grown sturdier in recent days.

I'm no match for this.

Amane had seen right through Mahiru's scant bravado and noticed the anxieties she hadn't been able to shake. Anticipating this, he had manufactured a situation where she wouldn't protest.

He'd made it so Mahiru could automatically feel at ease.

Amane respected Mahiru's wishes above all, and he wasn't going to try to force her to tell him what was weighing on her mind. Mahiru let out a quiet sigh.

Really, this is just another thing I love about him.

Looking at her parents, Mahiru had once doubted the whole concept of a family.

It was no wonder that, to Mahiru, the idea of a close family was a fantasy, one she doubted existed in reality, but—whenever she was looking at Amane, it really made her feel she had a family that loved and respected each other, someone with whom she could grasp hands and build a life together.

She was desperately jealous of him—this boy who was raised in an ideal family. He was dazzling to look at.

…Amane is the one.

Mahiru, who had been born into a family that even a child could feel was worthless, had never much cared for the idea of spending her life with someone else or building her own family, But since meeting Amane, he'd taught her to have hope.

Gently wrapped up in Amane's tender love, Mahiru was reassured that, with this person, she could walk the path ahead and be happy.

Having thought that far ahead, she realized that, when she really considered it, she was totally willing to have that kind of relationship with Amane in the future, and without meaning to, she wriggled a little in his arms.

I definitely love him, and I never want to be apart from him again, but—!

Those were undoubtedly heavy thoughts for a high school student.

She knew perfectly well that the vast majority of normal high school romances only lasted so long, so it was probably a little, or maybe a lot, too serious to be thinking about setting her eyes on the future.

Though she knew Amane also loved her deeply, and she could see he wanted to be with her for a long time, it was almost unreasonably serious of her to be considering marriage at this point.

She groaned quietly, bewildered by the intensity of her own attachment and affection for him, but of course, Amane didn't have any way of knowing the chaos that was in Mahiru's heart, and he just gently stroked her back like he was worried about her.

"...Um...Amane?"

"Hm?"

"...Isn't it heavy?"

He didn't ask her what, but he was probably clever enough to know.

After blinking several times at Mahiru's question, Amane smiled like he found it funny.

"You don't need to worry about that; you're not heavy. I have been working out, you know. Are you really that anxious about it?"

"I'm not exactly anxious—"

"You worry about the littlest things, Mahiru. You should quit worrying and let me spoil you for once. You can depend on me. Lean on me. If it helps you calm down even a little, I'll take anything

©Hanekoto

you dish out. You're restrained about the funniest things." Amane laughed.

He seemed to have picked up on the double meaning of her word *heavy*.

Mahiru hadn't said anything about the other meaning, the true meaning, of *heavy*, so he might not actually have known. But for Mahiru, his answer was perfect.

Amane accepted her, and that was all she needed.

"Um, so listen, if you're ever having a hard time, or if you're overwhelmed by anxiety, please say something. I mean, I probably won't be able to do much about whatever's causing it, and I can't exactly take on your suffering for you…but what I can do is be by your side for as long as you need. I can stay with you until you make it out the other side."

"…Okay."

"If things will get easier if you vent, you can vent to me, or if you'd rather not talk about them, you don't have to. I'll accept whatever makes things easier for you."

She could count on Amane to respect her wishes. From the bottom of her heart, she felt glad she had fallen in love with this person, as she let her body relax into his.

"…I'm all right."

She wasn't planning to talk about her parents with Amane again. She'd already done that the other day.

She was sure she wouldn't be able to fully process this jumble of gray feelings all on her own.

However, with Amane by her side, Mahiru felt like she could accept the negative emotions and memories that were lurking deep inside her and move forward.

"Listen, it's not about putting on a brave front or holding on to grudges… This is something that I have to grapple with in order to be able to move forward, I think."

The frustrations and sorrows of her younger self had poured forth seemingly without end, no matter how much she had vented.

In the end, as long as nothing really changed, even if she did share those feelings, they would just come back again someday.

In order to move forward with Amane, she would need to digest and release the warped ideas surrounding parental relationships that had been hammered into her heart from a young age by her unfulfilled yearning for her parents' love.

So that she would not make any more mistakes.

"…Okay."

Amane responded quietly and rubbed Mahiru's back.

"Just having you by my side is enough. I feel like your presence is what's keeping me afloat."

"That's a real overstatement."

"It's true, you know?"

If Amane wasn't around, if she had never met him, Mahiru was sure her future wouldn't be so bright.

It seemed to her like she would never have trusted anyone, and she would never have been able to love anyone from the bottom of her heart. She would have gone on living shrouded in the hopeless gloom left in her by her parents.

Certainly, she would have walked through her life in solitude, under a cloudy sky.

"…I feel really blessed to have met you, Amane," Mahiru mumbled earnestly.

Amane didn't say anything further; he simply wrapped Mahiru up gently and held her close.

The More You Polish It, the More It Shines

After cleanly washing away the sweat and fatigue of the day in the hot water, Amane got out of the bath and returned to the living room, where Mahiru was sitting on the sofa flipping through a book.

It was already past ten o'clock in the evening, and usually she would have gone home by that time, but for some reason, she was still there.

She usually went home for the night right around the time Amane got in the bath, so right before he got in, he'd said good night to her and assumed she'd be gone by the time he got out.

"Oh, you haven't gone home yet? I was sure you would've left already."

He didn't mind her staying later. After all, she lived next door, and they were dating.

The only thing Amane was worried about was that Mahiru might have stuff she needed to take care of at home.

She had probably already done whatever she could get done there at Amane's place, and she was probably going to come right back after taking her own bath at home, but still he wondered whether there might be other parts of her daily routine or tasks that he wasn't aware of.

"Sorry, I meant to go home before you got out of your bath, Amane, but...I thought I'd get to a good stopping place first."

Apparently she had gotten absorbed in completing her workbook.

Since Mahiru always managed to finish learning everything they were studying in high school ahead of time, she never had to cram like other students. But since she was a deeply serious student and a hard worker, Mahiru never failed to review the material anyway.

She had probably already memorized the contents of that particular workbook, but perhaps she was working through the book again to etch everything securely into her mind.

"Wow, you're a real go-getter. Good job."

"Why, thank you."

Sitting next to her on the couch, he patted Mahiru on the head, and she narrowed her eyes as if it tickled. He thought about combing his fingers through her hair, but he gave up on the idea because he realized it might catch in her dry hair since he had just gotten out of the bath, and he might mess it up.

Mahiru seemed a bit dissatisfied. Chuckling quietly to himself about how easy she had become to read, he stroked her cheeks, which were puffed up and pouty, and the haze that had begun smothering Mahiru's spirit came rushing out past her lips in one long sigh.

As Amane gently tickled her cheeks, envying the care she put into her skin, he peered over at the workbook that was in Mahiru's hands.

It was quite far ahead of the material that Amane and his classmates were learning at the moment, but being the kind of student he was, Amane had already looked it over in preparation, and Mahiru had taught him the material while she was reviewing it for herself. Thanks to that, he knew it was mostly stuff he could understand.

Internally, he was awed by how multitalented Mahiru was.

"When you're done with this one, Mahiru, could I borrow it for a little while? I'd like to give it a try, too."

"That's fine. Actually I've worked through this book several times already, so I can just give it to you. I've got others."

"Nah, it's no rush, so you don't have to do that. Don't worry too much about me."

Amane didn't want her to prioritize him like that.

He had just asked on a whim, thinking it would be nice if he could borrow it, so he didn't mean to be pushy about it and put her out, and he preferred to turn her down rather than be selfish.

"It's really fine, though. I've still got plenty of other textbooks in my apartment that have similar material in them."

"…Seriously?"

"Don't make fun of me, please. The more workbooks you solve, the more you can polish your skills and master the material, so I complete them more than once and then buy new ones. Plus, I enjoy going through them."

She was totally nonchalant as she said this, and Amane could only feel bewildered.

Well, he understood having several different workbooks, and he also had more than one for each subject, but from the tone of Mahiru's voice, it sounded like she had far more of them. Amane was extremely impressed. He wasn't nearly as thorough as she was.

Amane also enjoyed studying. He liked how the time and effort he put in was rewarded with a deeper understanding of the material. Still, this made him realize Mahiru worked much harder at her studies than he did.

"…All right, then, I'll borrow it, but I don't want you prioritizing me too much, Mahiru."

"I'm not, trust me. I really don't need this one, okay? Besides, I can just work through it again after you're done with it, Amane. You're the one who's overthinking things!"

As though in retaliation, Mahiru started squishing Amane's

cheeks and tickling them with her fingertips. He narrowed his eyes and let her do as she pleased, but Mahiru suddenly stopped.

Amane wondered what was going on to make her suddenly freeze. He could see Mahiru was staring intently at his cheek…or actually at his whole face.

"What's the matter? Have I got a zit or something?"

As far as he had been able to see, there hadn't been anything there earlier when he'd done his skin care routine looking in the mirror, and he didn't feel anything, either, but perhaps he had missed one. Amane thought back on his face as he'd seen it in the mirror, and Mahiru let her flaxen hair flow loosely as she tilted her head.

"No, the opposite. Amane, your skin's gotten really nice."

"Ah, so that's it. I thought there was something wrong."

"Compared to before, your pores are smaller, your skin's not as dry, and it feels totally different. Taking another look at it now from up close, it just occurred to me that it's started to look really great."

"I can't believe you were looking that closely."

Until recently, Amane had been the kind of person who was indifferent to such things, so he was frankly startled by the strength of Mahiru's memory and her powers of observation.

"I'm glad to hear the results of my efforts are starting to show. I've been trying a little harder at skin care, you know."

"Oh, you changed your routine?"

"Well, I mean, I don't take it as seriously as you do, Mahiru, and I didn't spend all that much money, but yeah. I'm just making sure to wash and moisturize well."

After doing a little bit of research, he'd learned that being mindful of just those two things could change a person's skin a lot.

Amane, whose skin was perfectly average, not particularly poor or beautiful, had been washing his face and moisturizing relatively casually, but since he wanted to work on himself, he had changed his face wash and his skin care supplies after doing some research.

All he had done was try out a few different types, choose the one that suited his skin best, and reliably and thoroughly moisturized, but the condition of his skin had improved just from making those small changes.

Since he had also already started eating an extremely well-balanced diet thanks to Mahiru's cooking, his skin was almost unrecognizable, compared to before.

"Well done. Guys have oilier faces than girls, so it's important to wash and moisturize regularly."

"I've had it really easy, since you've been supporting me with good eating habits, Mahiru… I'm just trying to do some basic skin care and get quality sleep. It really must be hard for you, doing all these things as if they're second nature. You've got natural beauty, Mahiru, but you maintain it through an incredible amount of effort. I realize that now."

"Heh-heh, thank you for noticing. It makes me so happy that you understand how much effort I put in."

"I can tell just by looking at you, Mahiru. You're always trying your hardest and improving yourself, aren't you? I mean, I remember what you told me that one time. I think you're amazing for trying so hard at everything."

That one time, Mahiru had said that, for the sake of her future, she wouldn't slack in her efforts.

That time, she had said physical appearance was something that eventually declined, and she didn't intend to rely solely on her looks, but also that didn't mean she wasn't going to work on her outward appearance. She'd said she was going to improve not only her looks but her substance and her skills as well, and she was proving true to her word.

Once again, Amane was struck by how awesome she was.

"...Thank you very much. Though I'm a little embarrassed to hear that you remember that."

"Why? You're trying your best; isn't that it?"

"...If you think so, then I'm happy."

Mahiru mumbled like there was something she was struggling to say, and Amane wondered whether it was really something to be so embarrassed over...and though he tried to recall more of their conversation at that time, he couldn't remember anything else in particular.

He looked at Mahiru, wondering if there was something she was feeling nervous about, but she didn't seem inclined to respond, and she didn't meet his eyes.

Even so, when he turned his gaze toward her, she said forcefully, half chiding and half challenging, "You don't have to worry about it."

Amane instantly concluded that prying any further would only tick Mahiru off, and he apologized quickly, "Sorry," and drove the question from his mind.

"...By the way, if I may ask, why did you start caring so much, Amane?"

"Huh?"

"Well, you were working so hard at your bodybuilding, but you didn't really care about little details... I just thought there might have been some reason why you started."

"Well, like, how do I put this? ...Once I started caring about one part, I started caring about them all. When I started looking into bodybuilding and physical training, I started researching daily habits and skin quality and all this other stuff, and suddenly I was thinking about so many different things."

Amane didn't really have any intention of paying as much attention to his appearance as Mahiru did, but he was the kind of person who would commit 100 percent once he set his mind to something.

He had looked up a variety of techniques he could use to improve himself so he could become worthy of standing next to Mahiru.

Thanks to the internet, it was easy to find the information he wanted, although he did need to be able to discern whether it was true or not.

Amane had wondered how he could become more attractive as a guy, and how he could improve himself. Once he looked up some tips and carefully selected some to follow, he incorporated them into his daily life.

It hadn't been all that difficult.

He prioritized training the parts of his body that bothered him. Then he studied up on skin care because often first impressions were based on complexion and appearance. He even tried out different methods to get a better night's sleep. And he tried to develop his fashion sense by asking Itsuki and Yuuta for their opinions on what colors and clothes suited him best.

Needless to say, Amane was hard at work.

He wasn't putting in as much effort as Mahiru, so it wasn't really anything to write home about, but he was doing his best in the areas he had decided to focus on.

"Regardless of your reasoning, I think it's a good thing. There's no endpoint for self-improvement, so keep it up until you're more satisfied with yourself, to a certain degree."

"Yeah. Well, if it's something I can achieve with just a little bit of effort, then doing it will give me greater returns later, I figure."

"I think following through on whatever you set your mind to is an important attitude to have. It's impressive, really. I think this is the perfect excuse to spoil you."

Just as Amane knew about Mahiru's efforts, Mahiru also seemed to know about Amane's.

She knew he had made it through his jogging and weight training before dinner and he had further exhausted his physical strength by taking a bath. She put on a mischievous look that was also kind of alluring, and she spread out her arms.

Because she was wearing a thin blouse that day, he could see her swaying gently beneath the sheer fabric.

"...Now, Mahiru, are you aware that you're proposing something dangerous?"

"Come on, it's not dangerous. I'll just hug you a little."

"That's exactly what's dangerous, ma'am. Please try to understand."

It was one thing for Amane to hug Mahiru, but it was a big problem for her to hug him.

They were a couple, so it probably wasn't exactly a problem, per se, but it did threaten Amane's self-control. He had buried his face in Mahiru's curves once before, and it was an extremely pleasant experience, but it also put him in an extremely difficult position.

He stared at her for a second, wondering if she really understood what she was suggesting, and Mahiru slowly curled her lips into a smile and gently reached for Amane with her extended arms—and brushed her hand through his hair.

"...You just want to rub my head?"

"You figured it out, huh?"

Mahiru giggled in her elegant way. Amane realized she'd made a joke at his expense, and he frowned slightly. But Mahiru also seemed to find that funny, and she just smiled.

"You don't like it?"

"...No, it's fine."

"Does it feel nice?"

"...Why would you ask me something like that?"

"Oh, well, there are some things you might not hate, but you might not necessarily love them either, right? It's a fine line, but I thought I'd give it a try."

"...I-it's nice enough, I guess, but, uh—"

He enjoyed having his hair touched and being pampered by Mahiru. Those things made him happy, but he was also having some very complicated feelings. If he honestly followed his desires and really enjoyed Mahiru's hug, he was certain it would make him want more.

"Well then, what are you waiting for? Get over here!"

"L-listen, there's obviously an issue with the location. Are you okay with me sticking my face right there?"

"If you're fine with it, you can go right ahead, Amane."

She knows what she's saying.

She was proposing to hold him and dote on him, fully confident Amane wouldn't do anything inappropriate or go too far.

He looked at Mahiru, shuddering a little at how much of a wicked temptress his own girlfriend could be.

She probably didn't care whether he wound up embracing her or not. If he did, she would probably go right on petting him, and he could tell already that if he could resist the temptation, she would start messing with his hair and pampering him.

Feeling just a little bit frustrated by how easily he was playing into Mahiru's hands, he reached out toward her, troubled and hesitant.

"...That's not very fair of you," he whispered as he buried his face in Mahiru's collar.

He felt her body jolt slightly as if his touch tickled.

"Which one of us isn't being fair now?"

There was no way that even Amane was going to lean right up against her chest like that. Truthfully, Amane was a guy, so of course he would have liked to snuggle his face right down into those soft bulges and savor the feeling of them while she embraced him and he basked in her warmth.

However, if he allowed himself to do that, it would lower the barrier to the next level of physical contact, and he might end up doing something more, so for the sake of his own restraint and caution, this was the only way he could touch her.

Even this was really pushing the limits, he thought, as he kissed her neck and nuzzled his cheek against her. Mahiru seemed to have given up on her hug strategy and started stroking his head with one hand as part of her secondary plan.

"There, there."

"It feels like you're treating me like a child."

"You often do the same to me, though."

"I—I don't remember doing that."

"Well then, that's also not what I'm doing."

It was true her suggestion could be taken either as a way to treat a child or a way to treat a lover, so Amane couldn't offer a counterargument and had no choice but to keep silent.

"Good boy."

"…Okay, now there's no way you're not treating me like a little kid."

"It's a troubling thought, that complimenting you means I'm treating you like a kid."

"And your tone of voice?"

"I'm not even sure how to answer that."

It made him feel strange when she whispered to him in a voice filled with sweet affection, like one would use when while doting on a child, so Amane used the hand he had wrapped around Mahiru's back to playfully swat at her and register his discontent.

But as if to say she didn't care about such things at all, Mahiru gently ran her fingers through Amane's hair and touched him in an earnestly doting way.

"Please don't try to spoil me."

"Uh, no."

"What do you mean, no?"

"I need to show appreciation for your hard work, and there ought to be rewards for good effort."

"E-even so… Hey, listen—"

Mentally pointing out that the suggestion she had just made was problematic, Amane raised his head.

There was no denying the feeling that what was supposed to be Amane's reward time was turning into a reward for Mahiru. Or rather, that's what it actually already was, and when he pulled away from Mahiru's body, she let out a very reluctant sound of disappointment.

While he was cooling his thoroughly flushed cheeks, Amane stealthily peeked at Mahiru's face.

"So, hey, I only recently started trying so hard, after seeing how hard you always work. You never fail to put in all of this effort, and you work so much harder than I do, so if you're going to praise me for it, then you should praise yourself as well."

Naturally, it was difficult for Amane to suggest the same kind of reward time as she had just offered him, but leaving that aside, he thought he ought to commend Mahiru again and he needed to pamper her, too.

If he heaped praise onto her like he wanted to, Mahiru would be overwhelmed and would briefly stop doing the sort of thing she was doing at the moment, which was also part of his motivation.

"I always think you're amazing for working so hard at everything, Mahiru. You just reminded me again that I need to be working hard like this every day to improve myself. You always do it like it's a matter of course, but I know it's not that simple. And on top of everything, you do your studies, your housework, and your grooming, too, right? Seriously, I respect that."

At the moment, he was complimenting Mahiru with a certain aim in mind, but everything he had said and the feelings behind it were all true.

Except for bathing and sleeping, Amane spent most of his time with Mahiru, and their conversation had once again reminded him of the amount of effort that she put in.

She did it all calmly, as if it were a matter of course, but it certainly required a considerable amount of effort. Amane more or less tried to keep up with the housework, since it was his place and all, and thanks to that, he'd probably reduced her burden from how it once was. But even so, Mahiru had her own apartment to look after, which must have been quite a lot of work.

And yet she didn't seem unhappy about it, and she kept on working and improving herself. For Amane, it was dazzling to see her that way, and he couldn't help but respect her for doing it, and from his side of things, he wanted to support her, too.

"Ah, uh—"

"I want to follow your example, Mahiru, and work harder at things... I want to work until I feel confident enough to throw out my chest with pride. If I don't, I won't be satisfied with myself, I guess is what I'm trying to say. I mean, I'm happy and grateful when you compliment me, but the stuff you mentioned is hardly worth praising. I'd rather you praise and pamper me plenty once I've worked much, much harder."

Otherwise, Amane wouldn't be able to keep it up.

When he looked directly at her and made this request, Mahiru averted her eyes. He seemed to have overdone it again, complimenting her so much, it had embarrassed her.

"...R-really, Amane, once you make up your mind to do something, you go straight for it... You're so disciplined."

"Am I? I think I slack off an awful lot."

"I say that because I can see right into your heart."

"But if you can see through me, you know that I'm a total bum."

"In what way...?"

What way? Every way, of course.

Amane didn't think he was strict enough with himself to really be called disciplined, at least not compared to Mahiru. That word made much more sense if they were talking about her.

Amane's stance was that he would do whatever he could while still leaving himself plenty of opportunities to relax. He had no intention of running himself into the ground.

That was because whenever he did, he felt like he was going to break either his body or his mind, and he could tell it made Mahiru sad.

Mahiru was probably only letting him keep talking because his health and perspective on things were in such good shape.

"The thing about me is I never hated myself, but I didn't like myself, either. Because I had nothing to be proud about, and I was really undisciplined."

"...If you're talking about who you were when we first met, Amane, I can't deny that."

"I know, right? ...I want to start liking myself. It's not necessarily that I don't like the version of myself that couldn't put any effort in, but the version of me who has goals and puts in the effort is more likable, right?"

What it came down to was that Amane hadn't had any confidence in himself because he hadn't liked himself.

He'd disliked the irresponsible, easily irritated, cowardly Amane who'd only ever made excuses.

Amane had started making efforts in order to become the kind of man who was worthy of Mahiru. He had overcome and let go of all the humiliations, regrets, and fears of the past, and he finally seemed poised to start liking himself.

"Besides, I want to become a good man, you know?"

"You want to be popular?"

"Th-that's not really what I mean. I've said this before, but I really just want to have confidence in myself, and a man who is full of confidence seems like a good man, right? And I guess I want to be a good man so I can hold my head high when I'm next to you, Mahiru."

"Amane…"

"Well, I've still got a long way to go, though."

He hadn't necessarily set his ideals too high, but it was still going to be difficult to become a man who was a good match for the girl who was smiling by his side.

But he wasn't going to give up.

He would never say he was doing it for Mahiru's sake. Amane intended to continue making his efforts for his own sake, so he could have confidence, so he could be proud of himself.

"So you see, I intend to work hard for my own sake, because I'm not satisfied with myself."

"Great. Once again, I'll support you becoming the version of yourself that you want to be, Amane."

"Mm."

She'd supported him before, but this was different.

The first time, Mahiru hadn't understood why Amane was working so hard, but this time, she knew exactly why he was working so hard when she gave him that extra push.

The idea that Mahiru had come to love Amane just the way he was had sunk deeply into his mind, and he understood it perfectly well, and Mahiru had even told Amane, "You don't have to work so hard; it won't change the fact that I love you."

Despite what she said, Mahiru had chosen to respect Amane's wishes and that made him happier than anything else in the world. It also made him all the more eager to become the kind of man who Mahiru would fall in love with all over again.

"Okay, I'll do my best. I want you to fall even more in love with me, Mahiru."

"E-even more than this?!"

"Yep. After all, that would make me happy, and you'd be happy, too, that the person you love is so impressive. I think it's a win-win situation."

He was glad she felt like she couldn't love him any more than she already did, but Amane was sure there was a possibility her love for him would increase even more once he became an even better man. After all, Amane's affection for Mahiru knew no bounds, so it was possible the same was true for her.

If he could get her to love him even more, he wouldn't regret a single ounce of the effort it took.

"...If I loved you any more than I already do, I don't think I'd be able to live a normal life, though."

"Well, that's a little dramatic."

"It is not, geez."

Amane was skeptical about whether it was possible for Mahiru, who had such strong self-restraint, to become spoiled rotten, but she certainly seemed afraid of that possibility.

Her expression said that she didn't want him teasing her, so Amane apologized and stroked her cheeks with his fingertips to soothe her before she started sulking. It wasn't long before she traded her puffed-up cheeks for pouty lips.

"Well, when that happens, I'll take responsibility for spoiling you rotten."

"...Because you made a promise, right?"

"Yeah. Make sure you remember this. Because I won't make you regret it."

Out of everyone she could have picked, she had picked Amane, and the last thing he wanted to do was make her regret that choice.

In response to Amane's clear assertion, Mahiru opened her eyes wide, then bit her lip hard.

"Amane, you're such a heartbreaker."

"Where did that come from?!"

Amane's eyes bugged out when Mahiru suddenly seemed to be suspicious of his motivations, and Mahiru abruptly turned away from him in a huff.

From the Outside, They Seem...

"Amane, do you want to go shopping?"

One weekend day, a little while after Amane and Mahiru had started dating—

When Mahiru showed up at Amane's apartment, as was already becoming part of her daily routine, he went to the door to greet her with a comfortable "Come on in," and Mahiru had barely even said hello before she made that suggestion.

Since she'd brought it up while they were headed toward the living room together, Amane guessed she must really have a strong desire to go.

Generally, Mahiru wasn't very pushy. For the most part, she didn't put her desires into words directly, like, "I want XX," "I want to do XX," "I want to go to XX," and even if she did, she would often preface a request with, "If you don't mind, Amane."

Since that girl had directly invited him along, she must have had a clear purpose for going with Amane.

"Sure, okay, I don't really have anything to do today."

After they sat down on the sofa together, Amane agreed, and

Mahiru's expression obviously brightened when he accepted her invitation, so he almost couldn't help but laugh.

When he saw her suddenly break into a smile, and saw how happy she was, it lifted his mood as well.

"Is there something in particular that you want?"

"Yes, well, a few different things."

"Gotcha. Leave carrying the bags up to me."

He was sure she was probably happy about the idea of going on an outing with him, but if she was after a variety of things, then she would need him to be a walking clothes rack to hang all of her shopping bags on.

Amane had put on a fair amount of muscle lately, so he got a little excited thinking how easy it would be even if her bags were on the heavy side. He glanced at Mahiru, but suddenly noticed a hint of exasperation in them.

"Come on, why did you have to say that…? I want to go shopping with you, Amane. The 'with you' is the important part. Do you understand?"

He'd meant it half as a joke, but Mahiru was reminding him of what she wanted with a smile, like she didn't want him to get the wrong idea.

Under that kind of pressure, Amane had no choice but to meekly nod in agreement. "O-oh, okay… Yeah, I understand."

"Good grief. There's something I want to pick out with you, Amane, so I want to go together, okay? I wasn't thinking I wanted to use you for a pack mule. You get it?"

"Sorry, sorry. That's my fault, for not understanding a woman's heart."

"Very good."

Whenever she scolded Amane, or when she got pouty, she would find some reason to touch him, usually by swatting at him in an adorable way that hardly qualified as an attack. He realized once again that this behavior of hers had gotten more frequent since they'd started dating, and he smiled but hid it from Mahiru.

After he had let her vent her frustration for a little while, she seemed to settle down, and when the slaps weakened into pats, and she had adorably made her point, Amane turned to face Mahiru directly.

"So what are we going to buy?"

When he asked what crucial things she wanted to buy, for some reason, Mahiru pressed her lips together.

"Mahiru?"

Although she had shown him her strong desire to go out shopping, the moment he asked what they were shopping for, she fell silent.

Amane couldn't help but be extremely bewildered by the abrupt drop in enthusiasm, and he saw Mahiru glance over at him.

"…Um, you won't cringe or get angry?"

Amane seriously wondered what they might be going to buy.

"I think you know there's almost nothing that will make me angry."

"Okay, then you won't judge me?"

"I'm pretty sure I won't. But for now, I think if you refuse to tell me anything about it, we won't get very far."

Mahiru was a very sensible and levelheaded person, so she didn't seem like she would go shopping for the sort of things that would make Amane uncomfortable.

And anyway, since she was saying she wanted to go shopping with Amane, it couldn't be anything weird, he thought.

And yet from the way she was hesitating to tell him, he guessed it was something embarrassing.

Though he tried to imagine something that wasn't weird, but that she would be resistant to discussing openly, he didn't have the slightest clue what it could be.

He tried to picture something that would be fine for her to buy but might also bother him, something that would make him have that reaction when she showed it to him. After lots of thought, he began to wonder if there was a possibility it might be lingerie.

But if that was it, he couldn't imagine Mahiru inviting him along without a hint of embarrassment.

That wasn't the sort of thing Mahiru would want anyone else to see, and anyway, Amane and Mahiru didn't have a physical relationship yet. In their current situation, and given Mahiru's personality, it would be unthinkable for them to openly pick out something like that together.

Which meant Amane still didn't have a clue what she might want to buy.

"…A-ah, well, the thing is…I've been spending more time at your place, right, Amane?"

Without making any attempt to resolve Amane's confusion, she started talking in a hesitant voice.

"More time? You're pretty much always here, except for baths and sleeping."

"Well, we're dating now, aren't we?"

"Yeah."

"And so, well, I—I thought maybe I could keep a little more of, um, my stuff over here?"

"Yeah, sure."

In other words, she wanted to leave her things in Amane's apartment, and because they would be in his place, she also wanted to be thoughtful about matching his decor—that had to be what she was getting at.

When he heard her unbelievably sweet and adorable request, it made him ashamed of the rude things his imagination had conjured up.

Without showing any sign of what he'd been thinking, he readily accepted Mahiru's modest, unassuming request without any hesitation whatsoever, and Mahiru, the one who had suggested it, went wide-eyed with surprise.

"...Well, that was quick."

"I mean, you're over here a lot, so it makes sense you would need to keep more things here the more time you spend."

Actually, even at the present moment, a few of Mahiru's personal effects were basically permanent fixtures. She'd left hair care supplies, several textbooks, pens and pencils, recipe books, and other miscellaneous things she needed.

He hadn't really found any of it to be in the way, and luckily, Amane lived in his apartment alone, which was spacious by any account. The apartment had been chosen by his parents, who were most concerned with security, convenience, and location, and Amane had always thought it was too much. But since Mahiru had started spending so much time there, he'd become extremely grateful for the extra space.

When he patted her head gently to encourage her and told her she was welcome to keep more of her things at his place, Mahiru looked over at him timidly.

"What is it?"

"...Um, c-could we get m-matching sets?"

"Matching?"

Mahiru seemed to sense Amane's confusion as he wondered what exactly she wanted to match, and she continued awkwardly.

"Right now, with our dishes and everything, we've got the ones from my place and the ones from yours all mixed together, right?"

"That's right."

Amane had stocked his apartment with really only the bare minimum of dishes he needed. He was living alone and hadn't thought he was capable of doing much cooking, so he hadn't figured he needed anything more.

He was happy to keep using the cheap plates he had brought with him from home, and some would break from time to time, or to be more accurate, Amane would carelessly break them, so there were fewer and fewer unbroken plates.

Since Mahiru had started coming over, they'd added the dishes she brought, and they had been using both sets, but even though they used the ones that were closest to matching colors, it was undeniable that when they were set out on the table, there was no sense of unity.

"Um, I'd kind of like to use the same dishes."

"...Right."

"B-but listen, it's not like you don't have enough dishes, so if they'll be in the way—"

"It's fine; let's buy some. The ones I have are just the cheapest basics, and even if we get more, I've got plenty of space."

There was just no way he was going to reject Mahiru's desire to have matching dishes.

"In fact, you probably know that better than I do, Mahiru. You spend way more time in the kitchen, and you've seen how clumsy I can be, so actually, I would like to get more."

Since she had a better grasp of things in the kitchen than the guy who lived in the apartment did, she must have known how many plates he had and how much space there was for more.

He had a feeling the reason why Mahiru had been hesitant about suggesting they buy a new set of dishes was because she wasn't sure about pushing her own wishes on him, and because of the question of where the money would come from.

As to the first issue, Amane was more than okay with it, and when it came to the second question, Amane still had about a third of the money he'd saved up when he first moved into that apartment sitting in his bank account.

Amane had never been very materialistic, plus most of his things he had brought from home or his parents had provided for him, so he had everything he needed, and he hadn't bought all that much new stuff.

Moreover, Amane saved a lot on food expenses, thanks to the fact that Mahiru usually cooked for them, and since he had the type of personality to buy only what he needed, he really didn't waste that much money.

Consequently, he had money left in his bank account, so it wouldn't impact his lifestyle to buy a few things.

He could never truly express how grateful he was to his parents, who not only let him live alone but were supporting his lifestyle, even though it must have cost them a lot of money to do so.

He wasn't going to go out of his way to tell them, but even if he did, he knew his parents wouldn't criticize him for asking about buying dishware with Mahiru. Instead, they were more likely to say something like, *"Preparing for your new life together is important,"* and transfer him some extra money.

"...I'm not going to force the issue."

"But I think it's a good idea; it'll feel more like we're eating together if we have matching dishes."

"...Yes."

The person who had suggested it in the first place was being shy about it, so in order to reassure her it was all right, Amane hugged her and rubbed her back. Mahiru quietly leaned into him and nodded slightly, seeming happy.

They headed to the shopping mall immediately, to strike while the iron was hot, and Amane obediently followed his girlfriend around while Mahiru told him, "There's a tableware shop I like in here."

To Amane, who rarely went out shopping like this in areas that were usually teeming with crowds, Mahiru seemed like a dependable guide as she pulled him smoothly along by the hand, giving him the sense she was very familiar with the place. Without pointing out her pace was faster than usual and she was bouncing happily along, Amane smiled as he followed.

The store they eventually came to seemed to be mostly focused on selling Nordic-style tableware.

Even at first glance, the store had a stylish atmosphere, and the chic music tickled Amane's ears.

The dishes on display were refined and simple, yet bright and beautiful, and had such elegant designs. They looked right up Mahiru's alley.

"This place isn't all that expensive, but they still have nice designs, and their stuff is durable. I use these dishes at home, too."

"So that's why you were able to come straight here. You wanted to share your recommendations with me."

"W-was that bad? I mean, if they don't suit your tastes, there are plenty of other stores—"

"Don't be silly. Why do you always think I'm criticizing you when I'm not? I'm just happy you showed me something you like; that's all."

When it came to dishware, Amane didn't have any definite preferences, so he was happy to have Mahiru show him what she liked.

If they were going to use the same dishes, then of course it was good to get dishes that made them both happy.

He had heard from his parents that compromising and being charitable was the secret to a harmonious life. Amane felt like it made sense for the person who wasn't particularly picky to give priority to the one who was.

"I'll be happy using the ones that you like, Mahiru; we both will.

After all, doesn't it make you happy to see me enjoying things that I like?"

"Of course it makes me happy."

"Glad to hear it."

He could imagine that if they had different ideas about that, things might become strained in the future. He was grateful Mahiru was, just as he was, someone who could enjoy the happiness of the person she loved.

Impressed by the magnificent foresight of his parents, who had confidently told him that if both partners were happy together, then the happiness they felt would be doubled, and who had always put that theory into practice, Amane squeezed Mahiru's hand, noting she looked even happier than before, and they walked into the store together.

On the shelves were many dishes lined up in neat rows, all of them of high quality.

Dishware painted with realistic flowers in pastel colors was quite popular, but Amane had never cared for it much. However, all the dishes lined up in this store were, if he had to describe them, decorated with stylized flowers made into patterns.

Even Amane didn't have any objection to using dishware with such clean lines and tasteful colors.

"I want to narrow it down to the sizes we use most often and only buy those, okay? I have a tendency to pick up dishes with nice designs without thinking about it, but if we get ones in the shapes or sizes that are hard to use, then putting them away will be a challenge, so…"

Mahiru mumbled her words quietly as she carefully examined the many varieties of dishes.

"I understand how you feel."

He had similar thoughts about clothing.

Sometimes he bought something because he thought it was nice and liked the design, only to find that, in the end, it was a bad fit for the season, or a poor match for the clothes he already owned, and it ended up just sitting in a drawer.

Well, a big part of that is because I hardly ever go out anywhere, though.

Since he had never been the type to show off for anyone or try to look fashionable, he had experienced that vacant feeling many times, when he realized something he had bought because he liked it would just go to waste later.

And the dishes here were the same as the clothes.

No matter how much they liked a certain design, there was no point in buying things they wouldn't be able to use regularly. If a dish was an inconvenient size or shape for serving food, then he could imagine that after they bought it, it would eventually end up taking a position deep in the back of a cabinet, where it would fall into a slumber from which it might never awaken.

"There will be two of us using one of each dish, so we've got to take the size of the dining table and everything else into account, okay?"

"My table isn't all that big, yeah."

One more issue to consider was the width of the place where the plates would sit.

Frankly, the dining table at Amane's place was meant for one to two people. After all, he didn't invite people over, so he'd purchased a compact table that gave him no problems when he was alone. But now that decision was backfiring.

"Now I think a slightly bigger table would be better, but at the time I picked it, I was on my own."

"Well, eventually maybe we should think about buying a bigger one. For now, we'll make do."

"Yeah, you're right."

If the little table annoyed them in the future, they could always consider buying a replacement. Tucking that thought into a corner of his mind, Amane moved through the shop, keeping pace with Mahiru.

This was one of Mahiru's favorite stores, and she stopped frequently to evaluate the wares meticulously, so they weren't readily making any decisions.

"Hmm, they're all so good, I can't choose!"

"I'm glad you seem to be enjoying yourself."

"I really enjoy it when we go out together, but you know, I always worry I'll be having so much fun, I'll forget myself and grab your hand over nothing."

"I think that's okay now and then since you're normally so restrained."

"Absolutely not. If I hold your hand, there's a very good chance I'll forget what our original objective was, so I need you to make sure that doesn't happen, Amane."

"Leave it to me."

He doubted whether he would ever need to fulfill that duty, given Mahiru's level of self-control, but he went ahead and agreed.

Mahiru seemed even more pleased after he gave that answer, and she seemed cheerful as she entered into a decision-making mode, comparing plates that were all not exactly right. As her boyfriend, Amane watched her with a heedless smile on his face, finding her incredibly adorable when she was like that.

At times like this one, he thought it might be poor form not to give his own opinion, but he had no intention of putting a damper on Mahiru when she was enjoying herself so much.

In a good mood, she mumbled to no one in particular, "This might look good at home," and placed a simple flat plate painted with a pattern of small flowers and green ivy into the bottom of the shopping basket that was hanging from Amane's arm. As expected, she looked delighted.

"...Mahiru, were you this picky with the dishes at your own place, too?"

"Well, I'm careful to choose things I really like. To put it simply, it feels good to eat off beautiful plates, and ones you like, you know?"

"Sure, I get it. You kind of get excited looking at them, and it makes everything more delicious, huh?"

Even Amane, who was generally indifferent to most things, thought food tasted better when the presentation was beautiful, and he knew the look of a meal could increase his appetite.

"You could just eat rice, or if you really want to cut down on how many dishes we need to wash, you could set the frying pan or the pot or whatever it is right onto the dining table and use paper plates as serving plates, but when you do that, it makes the meal feel a little bland, right?"

"It makes things easy, but it doesn't exactly make for a pleasant table, huh?"

"Flavor is the most important thing, but presentation is also important, of course. It's just like with people—you start to form your impression from the very first glance."

"It's surprising to hear you say something like that, Mahiru."

He wouldn't have expected Mahiru, who was often judged by her outward appearance, to really say things like that, but she shook her head at him side to side, with a bitter smile.

"Cuisine works the same way. If something's in a sloppy heap, you won't feel very hungry for it, right? And if no one eats what you're serving, they won't know what it tastes like, will they?"

"Well, I guess that's true, but—"

"And humans are the same. If someone makes a good first impression, you'll be more inclined to get involved with them, and it will become easier for them to get to know what you're like on the inside. Although in that case, it's more a question of looking decent rather than being pretty or having a cute aesthetic. No one wants to have much to do with people who don't do the minimum to maintain their outward appearance—isn't that right?"

"Uh..."

"Why do you look like that was painful?"

"Well, because, until a little while ago, I was someone who didn't care about my looks."

Until Amane had begun making his efforts to keep up with Mahiru, he had been indifferent to his appearance.

He'd figured everything was fine as long as he wasn't unhygienic, and he had been lazy about ironing his clothes, had let his bangs grow out, and consequently had cultivated a gloomy sort of presence. He hadn't been unsanitary, but now he could look back and see his appearance hadn't been at all pleasant, either.

"In your case, Amane, you didn't seem unclean. I just thought you were gloomy, and your room was dirty, that's all."

"Uh, you really did me a favor back then."

"Heh-heh, and now you can do it all for yourself, which is very impressive."

"Well, it's not like I could rely on you for everything forever, is it?"

"It's great that you have ambition."

Amane stopped Mahiru before she could reach up and pat him on the head like a good boy, and a look of discontent clearly formed on her face, but when he told her briefly, "We're in public," that discontent suddenly disappeared, and in its place, embarrassment colored her cheeks.

Amane preferred not to get his head patted in public, so he breathed a sigh of relief that he had managed to check her just in time, but a small part of him did feel like it was too bad.

"A-anyway..." Mahiru sounded like she was embarrassed about

what she had almost done in public, as she continued talking in a very shrill voice, "Having some lovely plates makes the dining table feel richer, more stylish and pleasant, so I want something nice. But we've got to consider your preferences, too, Amane."

"I don't really have very strong preferences, I guess. I said this earlier, but I'm happy to get the ones with the designs you like, Mahiru. I trust your aesthetic sense, and I also want to learn to love the things you love."

"...You've got to stop suddenly turning on the charm like that."

"I wasn't trying to be charming!"

"Geez."

He shot her a skeptical look. Amane really hadn't been trying to charm her, so he felt like he was being falsely accused of something.

Mahiru pouted with an adorable huffy expression that wasn't quite anger, and she grumbled a line he'd heard often enough before, "This is why I can't take you anywhere, Amane." Then she set two plates she seemed to have picked out beforehand into the basket, side by side.

"This one, or this one, which do you like better?"

One of the plates had a geometrical pattern made up of blues and yellows on a white background, and the other one had a beautiful mint green background with white plants painted over it.

Neither of them was too showy, but they had a beauty that would make for a nice addition to their home.

Aside from his clothes, Amane personally preferred bolder colors over pastels in his belongings, so he honestly pointed at the plate with the white background and the blue-and-yellow pattern.

"I like this one. How about you?"

"All right, then, can we collect a set of these?"

Mahiru quickly accepted Amane's opinion and returned the other plate to where it had come from, then she placed a second plate in the pattern Amane had chosen into the basket, so all Amane could do was worry she had yielded to him the choice she had been looking forward to making.

"We can, but are you sure you're not holding back? I'm okay with getting the ones you like, you know?"

"Why are you being like that...? I told you at the beginning, I want to make the decision together with you, Amane. I like both designs about the same, and I'd like it even more if we picked ones you also like. That would make it even more enjoyable when we use them, right? I also want to learn to like the things you like, too."

When Mahiru took the words Amane had said and turned them around on him, he really felt what she meant when she said, "I can't take you anywhere," and he had to bite back the embarrassment that came welling up from deep within his chest, as well as the happiness that outweighed it.

"...Makes sense."

When he quietly agreed with her, Mahiru seemed satisfied she had gotten her payback on Amane, and she smiled brightly and snuggled up close against his arm.

"Now, we've got a rough idea of what we want, so let's choose the dishes together... Is that all right?"

"Yeah."

This must be the joy of being together.

As he steeped himself in the delight that was soaking deeply into his heart, Amane looked at Mahiru, pulling him by the hand with a soft smile on her face, and she responded with the same kind of smile.

After the two of them had chosen the plates and soup mugs they would use together, Mahiru paused in a corner of the store that had nothing to do with dishware.

At a glance, the store looked like it only sold tableware, but it apparently carried all sorts of kitchen implements, including cookware.

In a display case, which Mahiru seemed to be drawn toward, were rows of lunch boxes and thermoses with colorful designs.

"Could we check out this section, too?"

"That's fine, but you've already got several of your own. Did one break?"

"...I mean for you, Amane."

"For me?"

The abrupt switch to talking about him made Amane blink his eyes a few times.

Mahiru continued, "You don't seem to understand what I'm getting at. Listen, you and I eat different amounts of food. I don't think you eat all that much for a guy, but you usually eat more than I do, don't you? I've been thinking my lunch boxes are probably a little small for you. And using plastic containers is kind of boring."

"Ah, uh..."

Ever since they'd started dating, Amane had been openly eating lunch with Mahiru, and she often made his lunches for him.

Whenever she did, she used one of the lunch boxes she had in her apartment. When they were going to eat lunch together, she packed everything into a two-tiered lunch box, and when Amane ate with Itsuki and the other boys, she filled both layers of a double-layer box with side dishes and rolled-up rice balls for him on the side.

Amane wasn't particularly fussy about what kind of containers his food came in, but since Mahiru insisted using plain plastic containers "offended her aesthetic sensibilities," he had been letting her do things the way she liked.

"Sorry for making you do extra work."

"It's not every day, and even when I fix lunch, most of it is stuff I made ahead of time, or leftovers from dinner, so it's not that much extra work. And after all, Amane, you do help me put the lunches together when you get up in the morning. It makes me happy to hear you say how good they are, so it's no hardship at all."

"Thanks for always doing it. I appreciate getting to eat delicious food every day."

Amane was fully aware he was leading a lifestyle most high school boys, who only periodically got to eat lunches their girlfriends made, would envy. Mentally, he knelt down and paid his respects to Mahiru, whose kindhearted care went beyond angelic and made her seem more like a goddess to him.

"Heh-heh, I should thank you, too, for always eating my food with such gusto."

Mahiru was very kind to him in all ways, but still he thought it must be a large burden, so there was absolutely no way he could tell her he wanted her to make him lunch every day.

As Mahiru had said, most of the lunch dishes were either made ahead of time, or she made extra food at dinner and carried it over to the next day. But the rolled omelets she put into most of his lunches, or rather that he asked her to put in, were something she never failed to make in the morning, and she was always cooking up some dish that needed to be seasoned ahead of time and left to rest overnight. Really, he wondered when Mahiru had time to sleep.

Truly, he couldn't express how grateful he was.

If anything, he felt like he ought to be the one making lunches for Mahiru. Even though he had been helping with dinners, she was largely in charge of that, so Amane felt like he should be the one preparing their lunches.

"Could I try making lunch sometime?"

"You?"

When he tried suggesting it, Mahiru put on the most surprised look he had seen on her that day.

"Ah, maybe you're concerned about my cooking skills? I can cook, you know, more or less."

After all, Amane was sure Mahiru was also aware he had developed some degree of culinary skill, but maybe she was still worried because she was thinking of how he used to be.

Even so, he had gotten quite a bit better, and he hadn't gotten a bad reaction on the occasions when he'd cooked for Mahiru, so he'd made the suggestion without really thinking about it. He figured he could manage to handle packing lunches, and to a certain extent, he did feel confident he could make something work.

"Oh no, I don't think anyone would take a look at you lately and be able to say you're a bad cook. Your skills have improved a lot, and your food is perfectly tasty."

"Thanks for saying so."

"B-but what's brought this on all of a sudden?"

"Oh, well, you see, I don't think it's that great for me to rely on you for all of our meals, Mahiru. Besides, I think I'd like to make food for you, too."

Basically, the burden on Mahiru was too great, so if Amane was able to split that burden up and take some of it onto his own shoulders, he wanted to do that for her.

Just because it made him happy when she prepared lunch for him didn't necessarily mean she would be pleased with his lunches, but if she would be happy about it, then Amane would gladly make her lunch as well. If he could create a chain of happiness by returning the favor and doing things for his partner that made him happy when she did them for him, then he wanted to actively give it a try.

"Is that a no?"

"I-I'm glad you want to, but…is that really…all right with you?"

"Is what?"

"…People will see it, you know? When I eat."

In other words, she was asking whether he was okay with the students around her judging his food by its appearance.

"Uh, well, there's nothing I can do about that. If someone says it looks gross, you can go ahead and blame it on me."

"The moment anyone said that, I'd think about keeping my distance from that person. I don't mind cutting off toxic people."

"That might be a little extreme."

He didn't plan to make any food that looked gross, and he'd like to think that as long as Mahiru was satisfied, he wouldn't really care if someone else criticized his cooking. But if that happened, Mahiru would probably feel like her boyfriend had been insulted.

"I mean, even if I stayed friends with someone who would openly criticize my lunch right to my face knowing full well that my boyfriend had worked hard to make it for me, they'd probably latch on to something else later and have more to say. Although I don't remember ever spending time with the kind of people who would do that."

"And I'm in no position to criticize anyone else, but you're very selective about who you associate with, aren't you?"

"It's not polite to say, but I think people ought to be selective about their circle of friends. I don't want to let someone who would harm me or the people I care about get close to me, after all."

"That's perfectly reasonable."

In that case, the deciding factor ought to be whether that person would cause any harm or not.

Humans were all influenced to a greater or lesser degree by the people around them. In other words, it was the environment around a person that built them into who they were, and if there was a problem with that environment, it made it more likely that a person would head down a bad path.

"...But anyway, Amane, I don't really think you would make anything that looks bad, so I doubt anyone will say anything."

"I wonder... I've been working hard at it, but—"

"I'm the one who knows best just how much better you've gotten at cooking, Amane. I've been watching by your side, after all."

Mahiru's complete confidence in his cooking made Amana feel warm all over, and he broke into a broad smile.

"Okay, then let me show you the results of all my effort."

"I'm really looking forward to this!"

"But I'd like you to keep your expectations realistic."

Mahiru laid on the pressure a little with an impish smile on her face, and Amane gently squeezed her hand again and murmured, "I'll have to try hard to live up to your expectations."

"Was there anything else we should buy?"

After she had put the dishes and a new lunch box into the cart and checked they had generally gotten everything they'd originally come for, Mahiru thought back over it all, to make sure she hadn't overlooked anything.

"I already bought a matching cup to go with yours."

"Mm, if we're missing anything, I'd say it might be cutlery?"

"Ah, you're right. Since we're here, we should get the matching pattern."

If they were going to use matching tableware, it would probably feel nicer for the two of them to use cutlery with the same design as well. Mahiru nodded at Amane's suggestion.

"Well, I said that, but the spoons and forks and stuff that are at my place have a really simple design, so we're already using the same ones, aren't we? If we're going to match something, it should be the chopsticks, and I wouldn't expect this store to carry those."

Since they were in a store that was mainly filled with Nordic-style dishware, there were a few token chopsticks around with cute designs on them, but they couldn't find any with patterns that seemed like they would go well with Japanese food or even any made from plain bamboo.

"We'll have to look at a different store."

"Yeah, we will. You know, I'm not hurting for chopsticks, but the ones I have now are all different, so it's annoying when I go to get them out."

"If you don't sort through them carefully, it's easy to take a mismatch when you're in a hurry, isn't it?"

It was annoying to deal with, so for the time being, he was using a bunch of mismatched chopsticks, like ones from a hundred-yen-store bundle bundle that had the same print just in different colors, or plain, straight wooden ones.

It would have been quicker to find a matching set if he threw away all but the ones that he needed, but sorting through them would be a pain, so he'd gone on and on using them all, and as a result, he had trouble when he went to take them out, plus the print on the ones that had been cheap to begin with had begun peeling, and the drawer where he stored them had become a chaotic mess.

Since they were going to the trouble, Amane wanted to follow Mahiru's motto of using quality things for a long time and pick out some good chopsticks to use. But even Amane knew that, indeed, if that's what they were after, the best way to get it was to go to a specialty store.

"If we're going to pick out chopsticks, there is a store here in this mall. Do you want to head over there? We'll probably even be able to find some to match our plates."

"Good idea. Ah, but your hands are so little, Mahiru. If you get the same exact ones as me, I think they'll be hard for you to use. If we buy some, maybe we should get different sizes."

When he squeezed her hand he'd been holding, he heard an obvious "Hmph" of complaint.

Certainly, he wanted them to get matching designs, but if they got the same size, too, it would be difficult for one of them to use their chopsticks, so surely there was no need for them to be the same in that regard.

"It's because your hands are little that they're a cute size, Mahiru."

"Are you sure you're not making fun of me?"

"I'm not. Look, they're small enough that I can wrap them up in mine, which is pleasing for me at least."

After initially letting go of the hand he was holding, he covered it from above and squeezed it lightly, and Mahiru's small palm fit right into Amane's palm without any resistance.

Mahiru looked back and forth between her hand, which fit completely inside his, and Amane's face. "See, it's a perfect fit," Amane whispered with a smile, checking to make sure the little wrinkle that had formed in Mahiru's brow had relaxed.

"…I'll let you get away with it this time."

"Thank you for letting me get away with it. Come on, let's check out."

Even if she didn't particularly like being told she was small, Mahiru had quietly accepted being told she was cute. Smiling inconspicuously at her reaction, Amane looked around, wondering where the registers were.

The register was located a little farther back in the store, so they started to head that way when suddenly Amane overheard two people nearby—a man and a woman who looked like a couple—talking familiarly.

"This one's all right, isn't it?"

"What?! It's so tacky!"

"Hey, come on."

"You've got to be joking. We're gonna start living together today, so we have to do a good job of choosing. This is special."

©Hanekoto

The couple was getting ready to move into their new home, and they drew close to one another as they picked up different dishes, laughing together as they chose.

Both of them were full of enthusiasm, and as they carried on a conversation that made Amane flush as he watched them, they placed dish after dish into their basket and laughed happily together.

Watching them do that, he came to a halt.

Huh? he thought.

Could it be that's how we look to people around us? he wondered.

The moment he realized that, the heat rushed to his face so quickly, it felt like flames might shoot out of his head, and he felt anguished, as if the surface of his face had been scorched.

The couple in question didn't seem to pay any attention to Amane's presence, and they promptly moved along to another section of the store.

"Amane?"

He wasn't able to look directly at Mahiru, who was peering up at him with concern after he'd abruptly stopped walking.

"...Hey, can I say something I just thought of?"

"Sure."

"...Doesn't this look like we're a couple living together that's out shopping?"

Keeping the question to himself seemed like it would make the heat get too intense and scorch his insides, too, so he attempted to spread the fire under the guise of sharing his thoughts. In the corner of his vision, he could see Mahiru burst into flames right beside him.

Mahiru was quietly letting little repeating sounds fall from her trembling mouth, in almost a musical rhythm, "Li…li…li…?" Her face was glowing with heat just like Amane's, and she used her free hand to cover it.

The fact that she didn't shake her other hand free only stoked the fire already blazing inside Amane.

Mahiru had been looking very strange, trembling and shaking in the shop, but after taking a moment and several deep breaths, she looked up at Amane.

In her caramel-colored eyes, which were so wet, the tears threatened to spill over at any moment, there was a vivid mix of embarrassment and confusion but, behind that, a glimmering blend of passion and hope.

"...I-it's s-still early...for that."

After she said that, Mahiru stomped off desperately toward the registers like she was trying to escape, dragging Amane along by the hand.

"R-right, yeah. Still too early."

Too early...for now.

Rolling the words *for now* around in his mouth while somehow trying to contain the heat in his body, Amane followed the path his girlfriend blazed toward the registers.

Say the Name You'll Call Me Someday

Fundamentally, Mahiru was someone who always spoke politely, no matter who she was addressing.

Her position on that didn't seem to change, whether she was speaking to someone older or younger than she was. She was always polite when she spoke with teachers and classmates and even when students from younger classes talked to her. She spoke to everyone the same way, from employees in shops to people in the neighborhood and even a lost child she'd encountered once.

That didn't change even when it came to the special people in her life, and there was no difference in the way she spoke to Chitose, her closest friend, or even her boyfriend, Amane.

"Mahiru, you speak kind of formally toward everyone, huh?"

Thinking how odd that was, Amane asked about it after dinner one night, and Mahiru blinked several times in surprise, fluttering her long eyelashes.

It was an incredibly sudden question, so he felt bad for catching her off guard, but the words had already left his mouth, so it was too late for regrets.

Mahiru didn't seem particularly hurt by the question and said, "I guess I do. I'm just too accustomed to speaking that way, and I don't really notice it, though." She smiled and took a sip of her tea.

"Is there some reason you're so formal?"

When he asked a follow-up question, curious about why that was, Mahiru calmly set her cup down on the table, then cast her eyes downward, as if she was deep in thought.

"Hmm… The reason is kind of hard to explain, I guess."

"Hard to explain?"

"Of course, the main reason is to sound polite, but…there's also an element of wanting to maintain a certain distance from people."

As she'd said, Mahiru seemed to be struggling to articulate her reasons. She must have felt Amane's eyes on her, because she let her eyebrows droop softly into an expression of uncertainty.

"It's like, to a certain extent, whenever you interact with someone, you get closer to them, right? Physically and mentally."

"Well, I guess so, yeah."

"I'm the type of person who needs a wide bubble of my own personal space. Even when I am getting along with someone, more or less, when they come too close, I pull away, like…reflexively, I pull away; you get it?"

"Do you dislike it when I get too close, too?"

"N-not at all! I mean, if I hated having you in my personal space, Amane, I wouldn't be sitting beside you in the first place!"

Honestly, he had known she would deny it before he asked the question, but she denied it more fiercely than he'd expected, so he was a little overwhelmed by it.

"Um, I don't really think it makes me super unfriendly or anything, but…I don't know exactly how to put this. I guess I could say I don't want people getting any closer, and that feeling comes out in the way I talk maybe? It's become a habit at this point."

He could understand what Mahiru was trying to say.

Basically, Mahiru was a sociable person, and she greeted everyone with a smile, but at heart, she was somewhat of an introvert who liked to spend her days in peace and quiet. In private, that tendency of hers was obvious, and Amane could tell she didn't like getting too close to most people.

Even when she was with Amane, she wasn't necessarily always brimming with a desire to chitchat, and much of the time, they quietly did their own thing. The fact that she didn't reject him, even when he was sitting close beside her, and was actually happy about having him there, was because Amane was a special case. She wasn't like that with everybody.

Amane accepted that Mahiru was sensitive to people encroaching on her personal space, and he figured it was probably something like her protective instincts in action. Using polite language was something she did on purpose as part of that, and it seemed to be like a defensive wall for her.

"I do it partly to keep other people in check, so it's really not a very endearing reason, I know."

Mahiru let out a sigh. With a grim look, she pinched a piece of hair by the side of her face and twirled it around her finger.

"I'm a really twisted person, aren't I?"

"As your boyfriend, I think it's incredibly honest of you, and easy to understand."

"...You're twisted, too, then."

"I'm flattered."

"Don't tease me, please."

As her face reddened, Mahiru launched a (weak) attack against Amane's thighs, slapping at him where he sat beside her. He wondered what exactly about her was twisted, but Mahiru herself seemed fully convinced it was true.

"...I don't think I have any genuine friendships."

With a soft sigh, those words slipped from Mahiru's mouth, in a more monotonous tone than usual.

"Of course I do have friends, but I guess I just feel like relationships last only when they have some kind of merit. I don't want to say people make friends only because they want to enjoy some kind of benefit from it, or because they gain something emotionally, but I don't think people stay together without a good reason."

What Mahiru was trying to say was a little extreme, but he understood where she was coming from.

Any type of relationship fundamentally had its pros and cons, and people got involved with one another after weighing those.

That was true for friendships as well, which generally continued (or didn't) because there were mental and emotional benefits, such as having fun or feeling happy or feeling calm when spending time with a certain person. If demerits such as distrust or discomfort with someone's personality, or a sense of danger outweighed the merits, then it was natural to end that relationship.

Some people did seem to judge their friendships by what could be gained or lost, but at the end of the day, everyone was unconsciously making decisions based on what made them comfortable or uncomfortable.

"I'm extremely self-conscious and embarrassed about this, but I don't think there are very many people who have gotten close to me with pure intentions, you see. I know not everyone is like that, but most people I've known have approached me because they thought I could be useful to them in some way."

From the way she had sighed several times while they were talking, Amane could tell her words genuinely came from personal experience, and that made his heart ache. Amane could clearly see

Mahiru was all too used to having both kindness and malice directed toward her, and he bit his lip at the misery of that thought.

Mahiru's previous friends had all treated her like the angel they thought she was, but hearing her talk about it brought home once again that those relationships weren't all pleasant.

"They either liked me because I was cute, or because they could get me to help them with their homework, or because if they were friends with a girl who was popular, it would raise their own social standing or something like that. I guess it was bad, like, there were people who wanted me as an accessory or maybe a trophy? There were some girls who pretended to be friends with me so they could pick up the boys I rejected, and stuff… Well, there were all sorts of people."

From her somewhat listless and dejected tone of voice, Amane could tell that Mahiru had really suffered in the past, and without thinking, he started stroking her head sympathetically.

Mahiru's voice and facial expressions made it seem like her anxiety was mounting just from remembering it all. Amane was filled with admiration for how much she had endured.

He was frowning now, too, so in a panic, Mahiru spoke up, a little louder and brighter. "Of course, there were also plenty of people who just approached me because they thought I was some angel and were curious about me."

But Amane had seen her expression a moment earlier, and he could tell she had faced quite a struggle until things had resolved themselves.

"Well, so because of that, I decided to treat everyone equally with polite speech and manners and not let anyone cross the line I had set for myself. If I acted the same way toward everyone, anyone who tried to force their way into my bubble would automatically be shunned by everyone else around me, I figured… It's not a very good way of behaving, is it?"

She had held her ground against people who wanted to benefit from her popularity or use her more directly.

Mahiru had had trouble with personal relationships, and she had mastered this as a secret to success and a defensive strategy.

"...Seriously, things have been ridiculously hard for you, huh?"

"Well, I can't deny the possibility that those friendships were seasoned by my own assumptions, too, though. If you said I was overly self-conscious, I wouldn't deny it, you know."

"Nah, after seeing how popular you were, I wouldn't say you were overly self-conscious..."

Since it was well known she had a boyfriend now, things had settled down comparatively, but up until they had started dating, Mahiru's popularity had been a terrible thing to contend with.

She had always had people around her, boys and girls both, and according to Mahiru, she also regularly received love confessions. Things weren't so bad that she had a crowd following her wherever she went, but there were almost always several people by her side, and she'd struggled to find the chance to be alone.

However, just like Mahiru had said, it was also true Amane had never noticed anyone who seemed to be particularly close to her. He could only tell this because he'd seen Chitose forcefully pushing the others aside, but the other students seemed to be comparatively superficial acquaintances.

"It doesn't bother me that much now, because now everyone around me is a kind and good person."

She smiled, and it didn't look disingenuous.

Their current class had a lot of comparatively rational and mild-mannered people in it. Even the boys who had argued with him on Sports Day seemed to have given up now and weren't going to try anything with Amane or Mahiru, and when it came to the girls, for some reason, they seemed to have assumed the puzzling position of peacefully watching over them with smiles on their faces.

Amane and Mahiru were able to date peacefully and uneventfully, thanks to the understanding of their classmates, so he was extremely grateful for that.

"Actually, at first, this wasn't one of the reasons why I started talking that way, but…"

"At first?"

"Mmm…how do I put this? I have a feeling if I say this, you're going to be more bothered by it than I am, Amane."

Actually, the thing that bothered him was that she was giving him evasive answers in a tone of voice that suggested the topic was extremely hard for her to talk about. But when Amane blinked repeatedly, not understanding the reason why she would be so hesitant to speak, Mahiru continued resolutely.

"…Using formal language, well, doesn't it make me sound more like an honors student?"

A gasp escaped his lips.

And at the same time, the regret that he'd asked about this instantly hit him in the back of the head.

"While the other kids were learning all sorts of different words and using them without thinking too much about their connotations or the impressions they gave the listener, I realized if I was careful with my language and behaved politely and gracefully…at least to the adults, I would look like a very good girl, right?"

Mahiru continued, not seeming to notice the remorse that surfaced in Amane's voice and on his face.

Her expression was very gentle and calm, and her smile was carefully constructed, like she was showing him that "good girl." Seeing that made Amane's regret all the more intense.

"Even though it never paid off."

Those words she had previously said ran around and around in his head and wouldn't leave.

"At the time, I was so desperate to seem like a good girl, to get people to see me that way, I didn't care how I came off. Thinking back on it now, it seems so warped."

Mahiru called herself warped without any hesitation, and after staring in wonderment at Amane, who had fallen silent, she gazed at him with a troubled and panicked look in her eyes.

"Of course, I don't have any such intentions now; I mean, now it's more like a defensive wall. At this point, I don't think about it anymore."

When Mahiru tried to offer him some reassurance, because she was clearly worried about what Amane was thinking, he wrapped her body up in a hug, to tell her she could stop.

Though she stiffened for a moment, she soon relaxed and leaned into him. That showed how much she trusted him, Amane thought.

"…I love you no matter what kind of language you use, Mahiru. You don't have to be a good girl anymore."

"I—I know that."

"Let it sink in a little more, please."

"…Okay."

Amane loved everything about Mahiru.

That included her good-girl persona. And the part of her that was strict and sometimes hard to approach. And the part of her that feared getting close to people but also became lonely easily. And the part of her that claimed she was twisted for wearing a mask around others while ignoring how guilty it made her feel. All of these were facets of the darling girl he wanted to treasure.

By no means had he fallen in love with only the good parts of Mahiru, the parts he could see on the surface. Amane loved her dearly, including the darkness she carried within her.

He gently embraced her and rubbed her back, trying to convey that thought to her, and Mahiru squirmed in his arms, seeming embarrassed about it.

Even so, she didn't try to escape and seemed to find his touch pleasant, which proved just how much she trusted Amane.

"W-well, um, I'm sure that probably worries you, Amane, but that's not all, you know?"

"That's not all?"

"No. Um, I was practically raised by Miss Koyuki, right?"

"...You did say that."

"Ah, I don't want to make you feel depressed about that, okay?!"

Amane nodded along, feeling a little blue when he thought back on Mahiru's early life, even though it wasn't about him. When she saw that, Mahiru, in contrast, got flustered.

"It's just, I guess you'd say I learned a lot of things from the person who was always by my side. And Miss Koyuki basically always spoke politely. Of course, part of that is because she was employed to be there, but…she did that with pretty much everyone. I thought that behavior was so sophisticated and lovely. I wanted to be like her, so I copied her."

"I see… From what you've said, it wasn't just the way she spoke; her bearing and everything must have been elegant, too. If not, I guess you wouldn't have admired her and imitated her?"

"Right."

It was a relief just to know that Mahiru's behavior wasn't simply so she could be a "good girl."

The more he heard about the woman, the more fully Amane realized how important Miss Koyuki had been to Mahiru.

It was easy to imagine that if she hadn't been around, the Mahiru he knew wouldn't exist, either, so of course she had been important to Mahiru. But seeing how much Mahiru idolized her, he could tell she must have been a decent, kindhearted person.

Amane had never seen the woman before, but he felt like someday he would like to go meet Miss Koyuki, who had given so much guidance to Mahiru, and even though it wasn't his place to do so, he wanted to go thank her.

Even though Amane had no way of knowing for sure, he had a feeling that if Miss Koyuki saw how Mahiru had turned out, she would be delighted.

Mahiru had displayed a tremendous amount of trust in Miss Koyuki, and that was enough to make Amane, who was grateful Mahiru had had someone like that around her, break into a smile.

As he keenly appreciated Miss Koyuki, Amane stroked Mahiru's head, and she allowed him to pamper her without resistance. Then a thought suddenly occurred to him.

Miss Koyuki had been the reason why Mahiru had started speaking politely, but her reasons for continuing were because she wanted her parents' attention, because she wanted to be a good girl, and because she wanted to build an invisible wall between herself and others, to protect herself.

In which case, he wondered if she could now drop the formalities.

"By the way, if that's how it started, does that mean you don't have any particular attachment to formal speech now?"

"Sure, I suppose."

"...I wonder what you'll sound like, talking casually?"

Basically, Mahiru never switched into a casual way of talking. Sometimes she did utter words like *dummy* and *geez*, but she was never entirely casual, always polite to the end.

That included how she addressed other people. She called everybody *Mister* or *Miss*, and she even spoke with Amane in a rather formal tone of voice. If someone didn't know better, it might sound from her word choice like she wasn't particularly close to him. It was easy to tell that wasn't the case from her tone, though.

"T-talking casually?"

"Yeah. Well, like…because you're always so polite, even with your boyfriend. I've almost never heard you talk any other way is the thing."

"I-I'm not sure what I should…"

He fixed his gaze on Mahiru, which resulted in her shrinking in on herself uncomfortably in his arms.

"Sorry, sorry, I didn't mean to put you on the spot. It was just bugging me a little bit; that's all. You've always spoken politely to me, so I'm just curious to know."

"G-geez…you dummy."

Mahiru head-butted his chest several times, half to hide her embarrassment and half to chide him for saying that. After meting out her punishment on Amane for a little while, she glanced up at him.

In her eyes was a faltering, hesitant expression. Amane felt bad for forcing her into that position, and he gently patted her on the back. Eventually, Mahiru slowly opened her mouth to speak.

"…Amane, I love you, you know," she said quietly, almost whispering.

It was a short sentence; it probably didn't take her more than five seconds to say it.

And yet Amane's mind went blank for a moment, and he needed quite a bit of time to process Mahiru's words.

He was frozen in place, still holding Mahiru in his arms. Her words passed through his head time and time again, going around and around until he understood them, and when he finally managed to grasp what she had said, he looked down at her as she waited meekly there in his arms. He moved stiffly, like a creaky machine that had run out of oil.

Mahiru, being who she was, seemed to have overheated, and her face was bright red, and she had stopped moving.

Only the blur of moisture in her eyes moved, her tears trembling as they reflected the light.

Suddenly, those eyes were filled with embarrassment as she realized Amane was staring at her, and they were quickly hidden by the curtain of her eyelids.

As he watched both curtains come down, her long eyelashes quaking, Amane playfully bit on her pink lips that were also about to close.

Though she had started moving again, it wasn't to resist him. Instead, she surrendered everything to Amane and melted into him.

It had been only a brief kiss, but when he pulled away, Mahiru was looking up at him with even redder cheeks and even moister eyes than before.

She looked even more lovable like that.

"One more time."

"…No way."

"Not the kiss, what you said before."

"I'm not saying it again!"

"Aw."

"Dummy."

Realizing how sparse her repertoire of abusive words was, Amane gently pulled away from Mahiru as she hit him with an adorably inoffensive insult. There was something funny about the way that Mahiru, her face still red, pulled away from Amane and tried to cool her head down, so he smiled.

"I, too, am in love with you."

"…You don't have to be so formal, Amane."

"Yes, ma'am."

He was stuck under her arresting gaze, so he apologized meekly, and Mahiru, without saying anything further, sipped her tea, which looked like it had completely cooled, and she attempted to continue her own cooldown.

Still, he knew it would be mean to provoke Mahiru any further, so as he watched her drink her tea, Amane also took a sip of his abandoned coffee.

The stone-cold coffee was supposed to be black but mysteriously tasted sweet.

"…Let me just say again, the way you talk to me hasn't changed at all since we started dating, has it?"

He began to reminisce now that he was calmer, but sure enough, he found it kind of funny that she still spoke to him so formally, and it made him smile.

Mahiru seemed to have gotten her own composure back as well and seemed bothered by what he'd said. She let out a quiet, cute groaning noise.

"I—I mean, that's just what feels most natural with you…"

"Yeah, I guess I can't really imagine you talking any other way, Mahiru."

"I think stopping all of a sudden would be hard to do, even if I tried."

"Yeah, I guess you're right, but…I was wondering if it'll always be like this, forever."

It wasn't that he particularly disliked the way she talked, and he was aware that she gave him special treatment in her own way, but he did have some reservations about it staying this way indefinitely.

He hadn't clearly conveyed that feeling to Mahiru, but he was already prepared to spend the rest of his life with her, so if Mahiru would have him, they would never be apart, and as long as she wasn't unhappy, he never intended to leave her.

He was feeling strange about hearing Mahiru talk to him formally forever, even in the future. Then Mahiru stared up at him.

"...Hey, Amane?"

She called his name with a slight tilt of her head, and it made Amane bite the inside of his cheek. She had made it sound so intimate.

"...Something about talking this way doesn't sit right with me; it feels wrong."

"O-oh, okay."

"...And it's...embarrassing."

Amane was sure he was the one who should feel embarrassed, but he somehow kept his feelings in check and tried to wash away the sudden sweet taste in his mouth with another sip of coffee. After watching him for a few moments, Mahiru gently grabbed on to the hem of his shirt.

He wondered what was going on to spur this charming gesture, and he looked over at Mahiru. With upturned eyes, she peered into Amane's face, her cheeks flushed.

"Yes, Amane, dear?"

The sound of her softly saying his name like that nearly made him drop his mug with the coffee still in it.

Generally, Amane thought of Mahiru as the embodiment of cuteness, but at the same time, she displayed a mature kind of beauty.

Her faintly flushed face, sweet voice, and slightly embarrassed expression combined to give her an incredible appeal that made Amane feel like his mind was melting. There was no way he could not get excited.

He could tell she wasn't letting it show through on purpose, because she muttered bashfully, "That felt even more out of place than before, heh-heh," but it was clear to him the look had more power because it wasn't deliberate.

"...That one's harder on my heart somehow."

"Wh-what do you mean?"

"W-well, um, how do I put this, uh...?"

"Well?"

"...It's really... It sounds like you're my wife or something."

He felt embarrassed to put it into words, but he had to say it.

Mahiru had frozen, maybe because Amane's words were so unexpected, and she seemed to be scrutinizing their meaning. The next moment, her face reached an instant boil, and she started whacking away at Amane's upper arm.

"...Don't have such strange thoughts, please."

"I'm sorry."

Even Amane was aware he had said something fairly shocking, so he meekly apologized, and Mahiru said, "Good grief." After slapping at Amane even more weakly than she had before, Mahiru started acting like she was puzzling over something.

Contrary to his assumption that she was uncomfortable, he saw Mahiru had put on a somewhat amused, teasing smile, and he realized he had accidentally given Mahiru more material to play with.

"...So talking that way makes your heart pound harder, Amane?"

"If you do it enough, I'll get used to it, I'm sure."

"Hmph."

Amane was absolutely certain she was going to weaponize it, and he gave her a warning. Mahiru, who seemed like she had been scheming just as he feared, didn't even try to hide her dissatisfaction, and she stuck her lip out a little.

"...So it's best to use it occasionally, as a sneak attack, then."

"Now listen here, Miss Mahiru..."

"I didn't say anything!"

It didn't seem like she had given up on the idea at all, so he thought about pinching her all-too-comfortable-looking cheeks between his fingers, but Mahiru met Amane's gaze and then lowered her own a little.

Her eyelids trembled silently.

©Hanekoto

"So that's why…for now, talking like we always do is best."

Mahiru also seemed to have inferred the thing Amane had been thinking earlier.

She understood it was "for now," and she seemed ready to stay by his side. Amane reached his hand out toward her and placed it gently against her cheek. "Yeah," he answered quietly, and he smiled gently at Mahiru, whose ears had turned completely red.

A Secret Just for Two

Mahiru was in the bath alone, hugging her knees.

That was because she was desperately trying to suppress the urge to scream as she thought about what was going to happen, and she imagined all sorts of different scenarios.

I'm the one who said it, but…

"…Today…is it all right…if I don't go home?"

The night of the last day of the culture festival, she had gathered her courage and said those words to Amane, and he had accepted with considerable hesitation.

Amane understood this was not like that time at his parents' house, that this time she was determined and wanted to spend the night with him, as a lover. Even Amane, who would have rejected the idea with all his might and a bright red face when they were first beginning to date, had agreed, though he had been quite reluctant.

In other words, that meant he was losing his ability to resist his desire for Mahiru.

Mahiru understood it wasn't smart for her to do something like this, and it was actually foolish for a girl her age, but she wasn't completely ignorant.

She understood what kind of urges Amane had as a guy, and that he was desperately trying to suppress them, and she had accepted that as a matter of fact.

If she was going to spend the night with Amane, who had been just barely managing to withstand all his urges out of love for her, then naturally, there was a high possibility that would commit certain acts.

She was well aware she might be devoured at a moment's notice if something caused his self-restraint to unravel.

Mahiru was okay with that happening, which was why she had talked Amane into letting her stay over.

...Although it's not like I'm determined to do that sort of stuff or anything.

She got embarrassed remembering what she had said, and she sank down in the bathtub until the water reached her mouth. Though she tried to blow her shame out with the bubbles as she exhaled into the water, the fact was she was only in this situation as a consequence of the outrageous thing she herself had said, and thinking about that only made her feel more embarrassed.

She had told Amane to get out first, and she had remained in the bath alone, in order to do her own grooming.

Really she was only doing her regular grooming routine, but it wouldn't have been strange if, from Amane's perspective, it seemed like she was putting some extra effort into it.

Her reason for pleading to spend the night wasn't something she could share with anyone else, but she hadn't necessarily asked just because she wanted to do sexual things.

She had wanted to be by Amane's side, to feel his warmth, and to make up for not getting enough of Amane during the culture festival. Those feelings were strong, but she hadn't meant to ask for the rest of it.

However, she also knew it was likely something serious was going to happen when the two of them got so close, and she thought she was ready for it, physically and emotionally.

"…Ahhhhh."

She'd been prepared for that when she made the suggestion, but still, she wasn't able to fully hold down the embarrassment that came bubbling up. Her cry of hesitation became a muffled groan and echoed in the bathroom.

Mahiru was a teenage girl, and it wasn't like she had never fantasized about such things.

She had picked up on the reason why Amane sometimes moved away uncomfortably when they were touching, and from time to time, she felt a certain part of him she knew must be there.

It was because of that, or maybe thanks to that, she could kind of imagine being loved by Amane.

Mahiru had never had any personal experience with such matters, so her knowledge all came from her health education textbook and some girls' manga she had borrowed from Chitose. She understood on an intellectual level how the mechanics of intercourse worked, but that hadn't translated into a clear mental picture of the act.

With only meager knowledge and no actual experience, the most she was able to imagine was having her body touched, maybe holding each other close while naked, getting wound up in the sheets—those sorts of scenes.

Even so, for Mahiru, that was quite provocative, and more than enough to fry her brain.

Whenever she thought about all that and more happening to her body, she couldn't stop her heart from throbbing violently.

When she unconsciously put her hand against her chest, she felt her pulse, pounding beneath hot skin.

She was aware the feelings taxing her heart were half nervousness and half anticipation, and embarrassment continued to burn her up from inside.

...I do want to return his feelings, but...

She fully understood Amane was an extremely late bloomer and a very cautious person, and she was well aware it was because he respected her that he hadn't laid his hands on her yet.

And she also knew the desires he had been working so hard to keep hidden stemmed not simply from lust but came from the deep love he had for her.

That was why Mahiru wanted to respond to him in kind, to yield everything to him and be loved in body and mind. To become Amane's completely.

But even though that was the case, she still felt some reluctance.

...I-if I don't get out soon, Amane will know I'm having second thoughts.

While she was in the bath hesitating and dawdling like this, Amane was stuck waiting in the living room. She didn't want to keep him waiting.

Her heart still hadn't settled down, but she told herself to let whatever was going to happen happen, and she got out of the bath.

After gently wiping away the water that clung to her body, Mahiru covered herself with lotion and also applied her skin care products to her face.

She thought it would seem lewd if she was too fired up, so she decided to go through her usual grooming steps to make sure Amane wouldn't notice that anything was amiss. She couldn't help checking over her body extra carefully.

As she checked to make sure her skin was as springy and smooth as it usually was when she got out of the bath, she glanced over at the change of clothes she had in her basket.

She had brought two types of outfits with her.

©Hanekoto

One was a knee-length negligee and lace cardigan set she predicted Amane would like.

Though it did leave her collar uncovered, the negligee itself wasn't made of see-through fabric, and it was cut just right to emphasize her figure. When she put the cardigan on over it, it would keep her from being too exposed.

She could tell from watching the way Amane usually acted that he liked this type of outfit. Rather than clothes that openly asserted her sex appeal, he liked conservative garments that were moderately flirtatious.

Indeed, he liked neat, tidy outfits.

So I really ought to seal this one away somewhere.

She glanced at the other outfit she had piled the cardigan set on top of, as if to hide it underneath, and her excuse for buying it surfaced in her mind.

She'd really gotten it just in case, just for that.

She had purchased it because of Chitose's enthusiastic encouragement and her remark that, "There's no harm in having one outfit for when you want to tempt him," but the racy negligee, or rather, underwear set, was no comparison to the other negligee and cardigan. It was something Mahiru in her right mind would never actually wear.

First of all, the fabric was see-through and was structured in such a way that if she shifted it just a little, it exposed places that ought to be hidden. It was much too flimsy.

She had no doubt if she put that on for Amane, he would think she was much too eager, and he would pull away from her.

There was no way she could even put on such an embarrassing garment in the first place.

Though she thought she had been a fool for buying it, no matter how strongly Chitose had pushed her, she also felt afraid of the part of herself that would put it on if it seemed like it would make Amane happy.

T-today I'll wear the one with the cardigan.

Feeling like it had been unthinkably obscene of her to buy such a thing, she looked away from it and picked up the normal negligee.

In the end, the normal negligee had probably been the right choice.

Amane was sitting on the sofa as usual, watching television, but when Mahiru approached, he looked up at her, and his cheeks were more flushed than could be explained by his having just gotten out of the bath.

He looked openly relieved when he took in Mahiru's appearance. She thought that was probably a sign he'd been worried about what sort of advice Chitose might have given her.

Though she did give me a big push...

Mahiru was really glad she hadn't put on the other outfit.

Amane definitely wouldn't have been able to make eye contact with her if she was wearing something like that. She wouldn't have even had the confidence to step out in front of Amane in those clothes in the first place.

She didn't dislike the look he gave her, a mixture of relief and a little bit of excitement, but she did feel awkward, standing around in her nightclothes in a brightly lit room.

Amane had seen her in her pajamas when they'd stayed at his parents' house, but those pajamas were just normal house clothes, and they had hardly exposed anything. Even so, she'd been a bit embarrassed, but that was nothing compared to how she was dressed now.

Amane's eyes traced back and forth over her, thoroughly taking in what she was wearing, so she shrank back a little bit. But she had put it on specifically to show to Amane, so she didn't hide herself.

"D-does it look weird?"

She knew it didn't, based on Amane's reaction, but she couldn't stop herself from asking anyway.

Amane seemed to misunderstand her question as a sign of insecurity. He shook his head slowly. "No, it's cute, and it suits you well. It's different from what you wore at my parents' house; that's all." As he said that, he was looking her over coolly, even as he was taking it all in.

"O-obviously it wouldn't be good to wear clothes like this at your parents' house, would it? And since you're the only one who's going to see me, I kind of…made an effort, I guess."

It wasn't quite right to say she'd made that effort for Amane exactly; she could admit it was more like she did it because she wanted to make Amane happy or because she knew he found things like this tantalizing.

She found herself squirming, wondering if those might be shameful reasons for her to even think about, but Amane cast his eyes downward, as if he felt embarrassed by Mahiru's words.

It was obvious they were both feeling embarrassed, and it didn't seem like they were going to get anywhere like this, so Mahiru hesitantly took a seat next to Amane.

She could feel him stiffen beside her.

But Mahiru also wanted to be in closer contact with Amane—she wanted them to be together—so she nervously tilted over to lean against his body. Her movements were clumsy and awkward because the anxiety and anticipation over not knowing what was going to happen after this was filling her body with tension.

Amane, being who he was, stiffened up considerably, but maybe because he was trying as best he could to act casual, he supported Mahiru without shrinking away, and he felt dependable and solid.

"…Honestly, I wasn't sure what I was going to do if you came out wearing some kind of amazing lingerie."

He muttered those words quietly, and she couldn't help but tremble for a moment.

"Actually I kind of held back a little."

Far from holding back, she had actually bought the lingerie, and had even brought it over, but there was definitely no way she could tell him that.

"Now listen—"

"But, um, I—I worried that if I overdid it, you might pull away."

That was why she had refrained from wearing the other outfit, this time at least. But it was possible Amane might have been expecting something like that.

Even so, she still would have been embarrassed to wear something so showy and suggestive on what was probably just going to be the first day of many staying over, so she quietly mumbled, "I'm sure of it," as she remembered the nightgown, or rather, the underwear she had hidden with her change of clothes. It occurred to her that she didn't feel like hiding it anymore.

Meanwhile, Amane seemed to have imagined what it might be, and the color in his cheeks got even darker.

"…I wouldn't pull away. I'd be happy you were wearing something for me."

"I—I wouldn't wear something like that, you know."

"Well, you're not."

"Do you want me to?"

She had heard a little bit of disappointment in his voice, so she asked him a question back.

…I have a feeling the excitement would be too much for Amane.

And not only in terms of the fabric and the size of the garment. More than anything else, there was its design, which was meant to show off all the parts she normally kept hidden. Mahiru was worried he might faint the moment he saw it.

He was probably imagining some sheer, frilly thing, and actually Mahiru also thought clothes like that were pretty over the top, but the item Mahiru had brought with her this time would definitely leave her exposed as soon as she tried to show it to him. She was certain it was much more extreme than whatever Amane was imagining.

"Well, I mean, maybe someday...um, if you want to wear it, that is. If you want to show that to me, then do it."

"...Someday...okay?"

"Sure, someday... For now, you don't have to force it."

Though she was relieved he did want to see it someday, she had slightly complicated feelings about how easily Amane had backed down. At the same time, she was grateful for his respectful attitude.

Be that as it may, she still shot him a look questioning whether he should really be such a gentleman, but Amane just tilted his head in confusion, so all she could do was tell him, "It's nothing."

Amane smiled at her a little and squeezed the palm of her hand with his strong fingers.

Though she knew that was something he always did when he wanted to help her calm down, because of the situation they were in, she seized up for a moment. But then the soft warmth of his hand quickly spread to hers and melted away her tension.

Wordlessly, he told her not to overthink things. A soft warmth spread through the depths of her chest, and her lips curved gently into a smile.

That didn't change the fact that her heart was pounding, but that was less of a painful thing and more of a faint feeling of pressure, a gentle sensation derived from both excitement and apprehension.

At any rate, the message that Amane treasured Mahiru came through loud and clear, and still feeling that happy feeling, she leaned her head against him.

Amane's eyes were on the television, where someone was droning on in a monotonous voice.

On the screen, the two hosts were explaining current topics in calm, clear, easy-to-hear voices. But not a single word they said registered in Mahiru's mind, because of the person beside her.

Slowly, Amane also shifted his weight toward Mahiru, but it felt less like he was leaning on her and more like he was kind of snuggling up to her sweetly, which was probably the right way to put it.

Both of them absentmindedly listened to a newscaster going on and on in a buoyant tone of voice, and quietly, the moments passed.

Mahiru's wildly beating heart got its composure back and fell into a drowsy, comfortable rhythm as she felt their combined warmth.

She was feeling the regular pulse of her heart, back to its familiar tempo, and enjoying the warmth of Amane by her side and the feel of his fingers, when suddenly, Amane's fingers moved.

Until just a moment earlier, Amane had been squeezing her hand, trying to calm her down, but now he wasn't just holding her hand. Amane had grabbed hold of Mahiru by sliding his fingers in between hers.

In his gesture, she sensed less of a command for her not to run and more of a wish not to part from her, and Mahiru chose to squeeze him back gently again.

"...Should we go on to bed?"

He softly lowered his voice and spoke in a tender tone, and Mahiru silently squeezed Amane's hand once more.

Amane didn't push Mahiru along or pull her along. She went into his bedroom of her own free will, hand in hand with him.

Though she had prepared herself for the worst, she had to pretend not to notice the nervousness and embarrassment that rose inexorably up inside her, and in order to do so, she looked around his room, which ordinarily she tried not to examine too closely.

Since he had gotten involved with Mahiru, Amane had started to clean up properly after himself.

He also had the advantage of not having many things to begin with, and his room was now really clean and tidy.

It may have been a sign of his personality, but Amane had very few decorations in his room. What stood out to her was the beanbag sofa that had shown up that spring. It tempted people and had made Mahiru its prisoner. The other thing she noticed was the stuffed animal on top of the desk he used for his studies and other work.

When they'd gone on their date that past Golden Week, Mahiru had tried many times before finally winning that stuffed animal, and here sat the fruit of all her labor.

Everything else in Amane's room was simple, and the toy was the one thing that added charm to the space, as well as a conspicuous pop of color. And Amane must have been looking after it, for it was enshrined there on the desk without a speck of dust on it.

"…You've got your stuffed animal very neatly displayed, don't you?"

"Well, I just make sure it doesn't get too dusty. I don't hold it while I sleep or anything, like you do."

"A-are you making fun of me?"

The thing he was referring to, that she held in her sleep, was definitely the stuffed bear Amane had given her on her birthday.

Sure, she did go to bed almost every night holding it, and she also took good care of it, but it was embarrassing to have that pointed out to her. It was like he was calling her childish, even though she was already a high school student.

"What do you mean? I have no reason to make fun of you, when you look so cute doing it. I'm happy that you treasure my gifts."

Mahiru couldn't protest, not when he sounded so serious.

"…I've been taking very good care of the one you gave me, Amane."

"Thanks… You didn't bring it with you today, did you? The bear."

"Well, today I have you, so…"

"…Yeah."

That night, she was letting her teddy bear mind her place while she was gone.

The stuffed animal she slept with every night was relieved of duty, just for the evening, because tonight, Amane would fill that role.

Of course, Mahiru wasn't sure whether she would be the one holding him, or the one being held, but in either case, she had come this far because she intended for them to touch one another and fully feel the heat between them.

Her chest had started to hurt again with the realization that she was in Amane's bedroom, but when she curled in on herself, for some reason, Amane covered the stuffed animal with a blanket without saying a word.

The blanket itself had been hanging over his chair, so she knew where it had come from, but she didn't understand the meaning of his action at all, and the thumping of her heart immediately overwhelmed her thoughts.

"…Is something the matter?"

"Ah, w-well…I sort of…felt like we were being watched, and I couldn't relax."

"Heh-heh, so it was bothering you, too, Amane?"

"Oh hush."

"I find that part of you cute, you know?"

"That's rich, coming from someone who sleeps holding her teddy bear."

"I thought we finished that conversation earlier, geez."

There must have been something funny about Mahiru's huffy

expression, because Amane smiled in amusement. Mahiru used her free hand to jab at his side and mete out suitable punishment, but Amane didn't seem to care.

Instead he looked at her with amusement and delight and love, so Mahiru couldn't help but feel nervous under his warm gaze.

It was the fact that he could see right through to this one childish habit of hers that made her feel more embarrassed than anything else.

She looked at him with her eyes narrowed, feeling just a little bit annoyed with Amane, who was ready to accept everything about her, but Amane didn't seem surprised by the look she gave him, and a gentle smile formed on his lips.

Then he softly caught hold of her little hand, the one she was using to attack him, and he trapped it in his big hand.

His grip wasn't forceful.

He simply entwined their fingers so their palms met.

And that alone was enough to make Mahiru go limp.

At that point, she resigned herself to what was to follow, and she automatically let Amane guide her over to the bed.

She didn't resist him, but once they were sitting on the bed, she suddenly thought about what was going to happen, and the throbbing in her chest grew violent.

…I…I wonder what Amane wants to do.

She glanced up at him, but before she got a proper look at his face, he let go of her hand, and she fell into his arms.

"…So is it all right if we pick up where we left off in the bath?"

When she lifted her head from his chest and looked up at him, she met his obsidian-black eyes, which were still gentle but also reflected an urgent, somewhat impatient look.

She felt like she was being swallowed up by those eyes, and as much as she was panicking on the inside, she replied, "Y-yes," in a squeaky voice. She knew she was acting just a little bit awkward, but that was because she was startled by how Amane's demeanor had changed.

Whether or not he knew about the turmoil inside Mahiru, Amane gave her a little smile.

As she was reeling from the shades of meaning she saw in that smile, clumsy fingers lifted her chin, and he gently bit down on her lip.

She didn't even have time to make a sound.

Lips that felt a little bit firmer than her own touched hers gently.

It seemed like Amane had started taking better care of his lips lately, too; they weren't chapped at all. Those thin, firm lips caressed hers, as if he was trying to soothe her anxiety.

The heat she felt in his lips was so much more intense than her own.

Mahiru had finally gotten used to kissing, but in an attempt to ease her tension, Amane gently placed his lips over hers and slowly rubbed them together.

That felt ticklish, but not uncomfortable, and indescribably tantalizing.

One thing she was sure of was that the longer their lips touched, the more she would lose her strength, like it was being sucked right out of her, and the more she would end up leaning on Amane.

She felt like she would sway and fall backward if she weren't being supported by Amane's arms.

As his slightly firmer lips pecked at hers, she felt something difficult to describe but akin to ticklishness, and she laughed unintentionally. Amane, who had been kissing her, also laughed at Mahiru's reaction.

Amane kept going, ever so gently, and his kisses got deeper and deeper, like he was trying to savor Mahiru.

The hot, coarse tip of his tongue slipped inside, and though he used restraint, it searchingly explored the inside of Mahiru's mouth.

Though she did have some experience with it, she wasn't really accustomed to that kind of kiss.

Even so, she wanted to accept Amane's passion, and everything Amane was doing to her felt good—Mahiru found it in herself to answer in kind, just a little.

Through their lips, the heat of their bodies melted together.

She was aware that her breath was coming out just as hot as his, and both their breaths and their tongues entangled as they exchanged kisses, indulging their joint passions.

Though her head was in the clouds, her body was extremely sensitive to any stimulation, and just the feeling of Amane's palm brushing across her back to support her gave her chills as an unfamiliar sensation arose deep within her.

She couldn't tell whether he'd gotten more skilled, or whether he'd been holding back until now.

Amane's kisses quickly grew more intense, until sounds began to escape Mahiru's lips, along with little sighs.

Her voice was so excited and breathy. She had no idea where those noises were coming from. The gasps for air she was making almost sounded hoarse, somewhere between a pant and a moan.

It wasn't just her voice. Her body also felt strangely loose, as if she had completely melted, and it yielded completely to everything Amane was doing.

Mahiru answered Amane's kisses with kisses of her own, while a voice that was so sickly sweet, she could hardly believe she was the one producing it spilled from her mouth. In response, Amane softly allowed one hand to start moving.

As he traced his hand over the curve of her waist, which was covered by her negligee, it made her body quiver for a moment, but she didn't want to stop him at all.

Though the feeling of his hand slipping slowly upward sent a shiver up her spine, his kisses soon laid a different feeling on top of that.

—At this rate…

If she let Amane do as he pleased, she knew where they were headed, without even needing to think about it.

And she didn't intend to refuse.

But her body reacted to the idea by trembling dramatically, and Amane's hands immediately let go of her.

Not only that, but his lips pulled away, too, and when she saw how he looked, wearing an expression that was a mix of desire and guilt, Mahiru immediately buried her face in Amane's chest.

She also grabbed on to his hand, which had been moving slowly and with great care.

"Um, I don't…have any intention of revising what I said when I asked to stay over, so…"

Amane must have taken her earlier shiver for a sign of fear or rejection.

That's not it.

It would have been a lie for her to say that she wasn't scared at all.

Scared of exposing herself to another person for the first time, scared of learning sensations she had never felt before, scared of accepting desire.

She thought most people on the receiving end felt that fear.

It was only natural. Giving her body over to someone else meant that anything could happen to her, after all.

Even so, Mahiru had made up her mind to accept Amane.

When she looked up at him from within his arms, she saw a shade of surprise had colored his expression from earlier.

Ultimately, he had been trying to take a step back from himself. No matter how aroused he was, or how much he wanted Mahiru, he respected her and was trying to wait until she was ready for him.

There was just no way she could refuse Amane, when he was so consistently kind and selfless.

She wanted to accept Amane's passion, his heart, and his body. She wanted to make him hers. She wanted him to understand that he wasn't the only one who desired his partner.

With her eyes, she tried to say that although the embarrassment was making her hesitate, her determination had not wavered. She looked at Amane with eyes that were a little wet from the intensity of their kissing, and Amane let out a sigh.

She trembled, worried his sigh meant she had upset him somehow, and Amane roughly brushed his hair back from his forehead, took several deep breaths, and fixed his eyes on her.

In his obsidian-black eyes, along with a passion that burned so brightly he couldn't completely conceal it, there also dwelled a twinkle of levelheadedness.

"So, well..."

"Y-yes?"

"Speaking just for myself, I want to make you mine, Mahiru."

"...Yes."

She knew those were his true feelings. Though it was vulgar of her, she shifted her gaze downward a little, where she saw something that spoke more directly to that point than his words ever could.

"...But the thing is...I'm not old enough to take responsibility, and if something were to happen, it'd be you who would have the most trouble. Well, of course I would take responsibility, but it's not like I can promise we'd immediately have a legally clear relationship."

Mahiru wasn't dull or distracted enough to miss his meaning, once he'd said that much.

"Precisely because I care about you so much, Mahiru, I want to respect you. I wouldn't want to get in the way of what you want to do with your future, or keep you from studying what you want. When

I consider the fact that I'm going to spend a long time by your side, I know it would be awful to ruin your life over a moment of passion and desire."

"...Sure."

"I'm prepared to walk through this life with you, Mahiru. But I—"

"You don't need to say anything more."

She understood without him having to say it.

Really, this guy is...

In all respects, in his thoughts and actions, he cared for her.

It wasn't as if Mahiru hadn't considered things at all. She'd thought about the fact that the act that was the culmination of their love could create another life.

Birth control wasn't an absolute guarantee. No matter how careful they were, there was no guarantee.

As slight as it might be, the possibility would still be there, and if they were unlucky, Mahiru would end up growing a new life in her belly while she was still a student.

If that happened, there were sure to be some difficulties with school, and even if there weren't, she would probably be slandered and criticized behind her back.

Moreover, her troubles wouldn't end after the child was born. They would have to raise the baby. She didn't want to risk creating another person like her, a second Mahiru.

What a lucky girl I am.

Amane had considered everything and weighed it against the chance to unleash his own desires, desires he'd been suppressing for so long, and still he had chosen Mahiru's future. She gently reached her hand out for his cheek.

"Amane, I understand that you respect me so much and that you love me deeply. You treat me with such incredible care, I...I'm a really fortunate person."

Amane was hot to the touch.

She keenly felt just how cared for, loved, respected, and treasured she was.

Though she had been filled with happiness ever since they'd started dating, there had been some parts of her heart she hadn't been able to fill for some reason, where a cold draft had always blown through the cracks, but now those spaces were filled up with the person known as Amane.

All the empty spaces inside her heart had been completely filled by Amane.

With her mind and her body, Mahiru grasped what a tremendous blessing that was. She was so happy she felt like she might cry.

Without even trying to suppress the euphoria that was arising within her, Mahiru put as much feeling into her smile as she could, and she put her own lips over Amane's.

"...And I love you the way you are, from the bottom of my heart."

Mahiru was confident that, in that moment, no one was happier or more content than she was.

As she was on the verge of tears, everything about Mahiru slackened, and this time a rain of soft kisses from Amane poured down on her.

Amane's gentle kisses lit up her body and heart like faint rays of sunshine, and he gently wrapped her body up in his.

"Will you wait for me, until I'm able to take responsibility?"

She thought about what he could mean by that.

Amane's voice trembled a little, as he restrained himself in order to be able to walk with her into the future.

Under the gaze of those loving eyes of his, which also had just a little hint of resolve and rushed impatience in them, there in his embrace, it was easy for Mahiru, too, to imagine how much pressure Amane was enduring.

As proof of that, she could feel the embodiment of his urges asserting itself, as if to convey to her how he was just barely managing to keep himself in check, because they were in such close contact.

Because she had glanced down, she had accidentally caught sight of it, and it made her feel embarrassed, but since Amane's determination was visible, she didn't find it disagreeable at all.

She nodded bashfully at her boyfriend, who tried so hard and was so patient in everything he did, then she buried her face in his sturdy chest again.

As soon as she did, she was greeted with the intense pounding of his heart, and Mahiru's own heart leapt, as if in sympathy with his.

"Until then, I'll let you take good, good care of me."

Mahiru smiled as she said this to Amane. She was filled with awe at how fortunate she was. Amane nodded with a satisfied expression and gently embraced Mahiru again.

"I'll treasure you," she heard him whisper.

Filled with sweet and mellow hopes, Mahiru closed her eyelids.

They quietly embraced each other, their steady heartbeats overlapping, giving the illusion they had completely melted into one another.

"...So, um..."

After she had surrendered herself to the sensation, which was similar to dozing off in a gentle sunbeam, she heard a quiet voice.

"Yes?"

"Can I say something pathetic?"

For some reason, Amane was mumbling and stumbling over his words. Mahiru smiled in spite of herself, wondering what he could possibly be hesitating over at this point.

"Go ahead. I'm ready to accept every part of the person I love, the cool parts and the pathetic parts, and any requests."

Mahiru was prepared for everything, and she loved everything about this person.

She beckoned Amane to her, and even as she puzzled internally over what he might be considering pathetic, Amane falteringly brought his lips to her neck.

She trembled just a little at this sudden contact, but it wasn't like it had caused her any pain; she had just felt the heat of his breath, and Mahiru stiffened for just a moment, then relaxed.

"...Um, well...could I...touch you? Just a little bit."

Mahiru blinked dramatically at his request. His voice sounded quiet and husky but unmistakably filled with passion.

As for accepting Amane with her whole body, she didn't think he intended to take things that far. With that in mind, asking if he could touch her meant—

Though the blood rushed suddenly to her face as soon as she understood what he meant, Mahiru looked up at Amane before her embarrassment had abated, then she cast her eyes downward.

"...J-just be gentle, please."

She liked being touched by Amane. Though she knew that it would probably give her sensations she had never known before, she didn't intend to refuse.

If Amane was going to teach her something, she was certain it couldn't be a bad thing.

Besides, they'd promised. They'd sworn to have all their first times together.

There was no way she could reject Amane giving her one of his firsts.

When she answered quietly, biting back her embarrassment, Amane broke into a happy grin, tugged on Mahiru's hand until they collapsed onto the bed, and covered her.

With the brightness of the ceiling light against his back, Amane was staring down at Mahiru in excitement. Affectionately, lovingly, yearningly, pleadingly.

Deep inside his obsidian-black eyes flickered a simmering heat he couldn't completely hide, and mysteriously, just being looked at by those eyes made her whole body hot.

Her heartbeat, pounding away much faster than usual, didn't feel like it was her own.

The hands that always touched her so tenderly and shyly were still reserved, but they moved with definite intention as they traced over her body.

She wasn't scared at all.

"...So if anything's uncomfortable, or painful, make sure you tell me. I'll stop right away."

He must have been concerned when his touch caused her to shiver just for a moment out of nervousness, because before he touched her bare skin, Amane looked at her steadily and very seriously told her that.

Unintentionally, Mahiru laughed at the deeply earnest look of concern he gave her, which was enough to make her wonder where the sexiness from earlier had gone.

"...As a girl, it would make me happier if you would do what you like, though."

"Th-that might be true, but I don't want to force anything on you."

In response to his word, which showed such stubborn concern, Mahiru quietly laughed and reached out toward Amane.

When she placed her hand against his cheek, flushed from nerves and excitement, he got even redder, as if she had added fuel to the fire, and his eyes opened wide.

"Everything you do for me makes me happy, Amane... Please, let me accept your feelings."

Even if it did hurt a little, if it was something Amane was doing, she intended to accept it. There was no way Amane would do something painful for no reason, and she was well aware a little pain might be necessary.

Her resolve had taken that into account, too.

When she stared firmly into his eyes and smiled, Amane moved his mouth around wordlessly and swallowed like he was trying to resist something, then he put the hand that had been touching her body on Mahiru's chin and lifted her face up.

She did have some idea of what he was going to do to her, and although she squeezed her eyes shut, she could still imagine Amane looking nervous but wearing a smile he couldn't quite manage to suppress.

"...I'll do my very best to make it as good as possible for you, too, Mahiru."

He quietly dropped those words on her after planting a soft kiss that was really just a prelude, and Mahiru gently lowered her hand from Amane's cheek.

She was convinced, body and mind, that it was all right to entrust everything to Amane.

...*It's okay.*

As long as it was with him, from then until forever.

Filled with such deep reassurance and euphoria, Mahiru accepted the hand that was gently starting to trace a path to places she had never let anyone touch before.

When Mahiru woke up in the morning and realized where she had been sleeping, she instantly pursed her lips tightly together.

If she hadn't done so, she would have ended up sending Amane flying to his feet. He was wrapped around her, breathing peacefully as he embraced her in his sleep.

After somehow managing to contain the scream that very nearly escaped her mouth, Mahiru glanced over at her sleeping beloved as she tried to quiet her pounding heart. It was already worn out from enduring such a shock so early in the morning.

It seemed to be early enough that the morning sun had only just begun to peek out, and the curtains were also closed, so the light from the side lamp that they had forgotten to turn off was glaring.

Amane, gently illuminated by that light, was sleeping with a truly peaceful expression on his face.

In his sleep, he looked deeply satisfied, and his face was a little sweeter and more innocent than usual. Just seeing it was enough to make her crack a smile.

From the outside, he probably looked like a small child holding his stuffed animal, as he embraced Mahiru with a soft smile on his face, looking greatly satisfied.

That youthfulness was adorable, but it made her even more aware of the gulf between the boy she saw now and the young man he had been the night before—which brought to mind all sorts of other things. She pressed her lips together into a line.

…*That's not good.*

The "not good" referred to Amane from the night before.

The previous night, she had learned all sorts of things, none of which she had known before. They had taught each other as they went along. As a result, her knowledge in certain unexplored areas had increased, and she had also seen new sides of Amane.

For example, she'd learned that Amane was much more dexterous than she'd imagined, and he had greater powers of observation. She also found out that, despite everything else, he was still surprisingly fainthearted.

She'd also learned that the urges he had been resisting up until then had been even greater than she'd imagined.

Just thinking about what she'd learned brought to mind once again the way his eyes, fingertips, and lips had tenderly touched her as he'd explored her body meticulously. Her cheeks burned.

When she turned back the sheets to take a quick glance at the

©Hanekoto

parts of her they were covering, she saw that she'd put her original outfit back on properly...or it had been put back on her.

However, there were a fair number of wrinkles in the delicate fabric, and red blossoms had been planted here and there across the skin she was so proud of, spots that hadn't been there before she'd stayed the night.

The marks, which she could see here and there even on the places that weren't covered by her negligee, were signs of Amane's possessiveness and desire, and definite proof of their contact the night before.

When she became aware of the marks again, she felt embarrassed, but she also felt like they showed how badly Amane wanted her, and she didn't want to criticize him too strongly for it.

She let out a frustrated, heated sigh and buried her face in Amane's chest as he held her.

Before last night, she had touched Amane only over his clothes, so she hadn't been aware, but last night she had learned that his body was firmer and stronger than it looked. She'd touched it, experienced it.

When she'd traced her hands over him, his muscles had been surprisingly firm. She could feel every little bump and dip, and his sweaty, flushed skin had exuded a strange sort of eroticism, a manliness that shocked Mahiru's heart.

That was precisely why she felt so embarrassed by the position she was currently in. But her happiness won out over her embarrassment, so she clung to him anyway.

...He was a real man after all.

Not that she had ever doubted that. She'd known it all along, but that aspect of him had been partially obscured by the gentlemanly way he usually behaved, and Mahiru had let her guard down.

She had since learned, in body and mind, that Amane had just been desperately keeping that side of himself contained.

When she thought about the fact that the hand that was currently curled around her back was the same hand that had explored her so thoroughly, her body grew strangely warm.

Once she became conscious of that, overwhelmingly embarrassment and a keen compulsion to run away began to clash with her intense desire to spend this happy moment wrapped up in the arms of the person she loved.

If Amane had been awake, they probably would have snuggled for a while, but for the moment, he was still asleep.

Besides, the light shining in through the gap in the curtains was steadily growing stronger, so Mahiru knew she had better start her morning preparations.

Although it was the weekend, her routine didn't change much.

They hadn't done anything this time that had lasting effects, so she figured it was all right to go about her morning as per usual.

After deliberating for a little longer while enveloped in the scent and the warmth of the boy she loved, Mahiru decided to quietly slip out of the gentle embrace of Amane's arms.

It was time to get dressed and make breakfast.

That certainly wasn't because she feared she would remember too much and groan with embarrassment and roll around on the bed writhing in agony—not at all.

Mahiru carefully got out of bed so she wouldn't wake Amane, and she saw that her negligee was a total mess. In hopes of getting rid of some of the wrinkles, she straightened it out the best she could without damaging the fabric as she looked around the room for a clock.

Then she spotted the mound formed by the blanket on top of the desk, and she smiled a little.

She put on her slippers so she wouldn't make any noise and then approached the desk, where she uncovered the stuffed cat that had been sentenced to spend all night tucked under the blanket.

The cute, innocent eyes she revealed knew nothing of the previous night's events.

She tenderly picked up the poor cat, which had had to spend the whole night without its master, and quietly she placed it beside Amane, who was sound asleep, breathing peacefully, none the wiser.

It seemed like he might be confused or upset that Mahiru wasn't there when he woke up, so she did it out of consideration. She didn't want Amane to be lonely.

Amane looked really adorable, sleeping peacefully and cuddling the cat.

There wasn't the slightest vestige of the virile expressions or the looks of unconcealable passion he had shown her the night before. He just looked like he always did. Actually, since she had seen the other side of him the night before, he looked even younger and more darling than usual.

I'll have to sneak a photo later, she thought, knowing he would politely refuse if she asked. Mahiru put one knee on the bed, lightly kissed Amane's cheek while he was still sleeping, and she stood up.

I think I'll make breakfast. Those rolled omelets that Amane loves.

She wondered if this was what it felt like to be a wife eagerly waiting for her husband to wake up. At the same time, she was embarrassed because it was still far too soon for her to think about such things. In high spirits, Mahiru left the bedroom and headed for the bathroom sink.

Someone Who Looks Carefully

This is terrible, Mahiru grumbled internally, without saying anything out loud.

She'd been feeling unwell ever since she had woken up, and by the time she had gotten to school, it was clear she was in pretty poor shape.

Her head felt heavy, like there was a stone lying on top of it, and she could tell her thinking was slower than usual. The more she moved, the more it felt like she was getting pounded by some blunt instrument, and from time to time, her lower abdomen added to the pain with a feeling like countless needles stabbing into her. To make matters worse, her whole body felt hotter than usual, and a feeling of weariness persistently hung over her.

Though she'd come to the pragmatic conclusion that this phenomenon itself was an unavoidable part of the female condition, she nevertheless found it extremely irritating that even her hormones were wildly out of balance.

Though she felt a little emotionally unstable, she was capable of keeping that in check, so as she tried to calm her frayed feelings somehow through reason, she sighed softly.

She wasn't sure she had any right to complain, since from listening to other girls' tales of misery, she knew she had it comparatively easy, and once the medicine she'd taken kicked in, she would be able to carry on without any problems.

If the pain had been any worse, she probably wouldn't have hesitated to go to the hospital, but it wasn't so unbearable that she couldn't go about her day. It consistently stayed within the scope of simple discomfort.

At times like these, she regretted being born a girl, but it wasn't as if she ever had a choice in the matter.

For the time being, she had taken some medicine, and she made it through the school day trying not to let her discomfort show on her face. When she was finally free, Mahiru single-mindedly headed straight for home. She decided to pass the time at Amane's place since it helped settle her mind, but…before too long, Amane came back carrying shopping bags and stood there staring at her.

"You got home early."

"Sorry I left the shopping up to you today."

"Nah, I don't mind. It's just, guessing from how you look, I figured you must have gotten back pretty early, is all."

She had gone home remarkably quickly that day.

When she felt bad, Mahiru really hated being around other people, so she'd rushed home, anxious to pass the time in peace and quiet.

Though she had taken another round of medication and tried to settle down before Amane got back home, it didn't completely eliminate her pain or take immediate effect, so the fatigue that had been gradually taking over her body and the dull pain tormenting her welled up from deep inside.

"I thought we could just relax at home today."

She smiled, placing her hand lightly on her belly to try to hide her pain and discomfort, and Amane stood there and stared intently at her again.

Something in that look seemed to be probing Mahiru for answers.

"Is something wrong?"

"No, nothing."

The way Amane was acting showed that he was mulling over something, but he went right into the kitchen to put the groceries in the refrigerator. With a feeling of relief, Mahiru absentmindedly watched as he diligently bustled about.

Amane briskly put all the ingredients away with expert dexterity, then turned around and called her name across the counter.

"Mahiru?"

Mahiru, who was leaning against the back of the sofa more than she usually did, suddenly sat straight up.

"I'm boiling some water. Do you want anything to drink?" he asked.

"Huh? Ah, yes."

She agreed to his sudden suggestion without really thinking it through, but whether or not he had noticed her distracted condition, he was looking at her with a gaze that was somehow even gentler than usual.

"Are you all right with me picking what to make?"

"Oh, are you going to treat me to your very own specialty drink?"

"That's right. Let me go get it ready."

She was grateful just to have him make her something warm to drink, so she left everything up to Amane. Mahiru wasn't particularly concerned. Honestly, it would have been enough for him just to pour hot water into a cup for her, because she would have been happy just slowly sipping it as it cooled.

Not wanting to move too much, she leaned her weight back against the sofa again and listened idly as the singing sound from the mouth of the kettle grew louder. Then before she knew it, Amane came back into the living room.

In his hand was a single cup.

She was just wondering why when he said, "Here," and put the cup into Mahiru's hands.

Inside the cup, which wasn't hot to the touch due to its double-walled structure, was a liquid that was light yellow in color.

It looked like there was something fibrous mixed into it, but Mahiru had been spaced out and not really watching what Amane was making, so she didn't know what the cup contained.

When she tilted the cup a little, she could see it was a little thick from the way it moved around. Maybe because he had been stirring it until just a moment earlier, the mysterious fibers danced around in the cup, forming whirlpools that swirled around and around like clothes that had been tossed into a washing machine.

"…What's this?"

"Honey ginger tea. Ginger and honey are both good for the body, and they'll warm you up."

He said that and gently placed the blanket that had been hanging on the back of one of the dining room chairs around Mahiru's shoulders, then placed an unfamiliar bag on Mahiru's lap. She was completely bewildered by his actions.

In addition to the gentle warmth coming through the cup into her hands, she felt heat and warmth sinking into her lap, but even when Mahiru looked up at Amane questioningly, he kept the same calm expression.

"Hold it against your stomach."

She almost shouted when she realized the mysterious bag was a hot water bottle.

From the weight of it and the noise it made when she tilted it, she could tell it was filled with hot water.

Earlier, when he'd said he was "boiling some water," that must have actually been for the hot water bottle. The fact she didn't even see a drink for Amane himself in the kitchen meant he had been solely preparing the hot water bottle and a drink for Mahiru.

Amane sat down beside her, leaving a little space, and his face wasn't all that serious; his expression was simply flat, with a slight shade of concern in his eyes.

"It's better for you to be in a comfortable position. After you drink that, do you want to lie down?"

"N-no, I don't need—"

"In that case, maybe you can stay like this for now. If it gets too uncomfortable, let me know."

Amane smoothly indicated he had noticed she was in bad shape, and he picked up the remote control for the air conditioner and adjusted the temperature, which made her aware he had completely seen right through her.

"But h-how did you know?"

"…Something about the way you were behaving told me you weren't feeling well. Plus, you had your hand on your stomach. Once I noticed you feeling bad on a regular basis, I more or less figured it out, I guess."

Amane explained himself awkwardly, looking guilty for some reason.

Mahiru felt like she was the one who was guilty, for not only letting him become aware of what was going on, but making him worry about her. But Amane was the one who seemed to be anxious about something.

"S-sorry if that's creepy."

"Why would you say something like that?"

"Well, like, you might think it was c-creepy for a guy to know about something like that and make a fuss over you, or something."

There were some people who hated when others were overly considerate, and others would have been upset someone had noticed at all, so now that he'd said that, Mahiru perfectly understood Amane's hesitation.

As for Mahiru, though she was quite surprised Amane had noticed, she wasn't bothered by it, and she accepted his explanation.

And anyway, she'd been spending a lot of time with Amane, and since she'd fallen for him, she was generally at his place after school was over for the day. It wouldn't be an exaggeration to say that, except for baths and sleeping time, she was almost always at Amane's apartment.

Given that they spent so much time together, of course it wasn't strange that he had realized where her periodic bouts of poor health came from.

She understood Amane's worry that she might evade the topic, but knowing Amane had been paying attention to her made Mahiru reassured more than anything else.

"...It wouldn't feel very good if a stranger knew about it, but I don't really mind you knowing, Amane, not when we spend so much time together. I probably slipped up and made a face or something."

"You were trying not to let it show?"

"The pain itself comes every month, so that's an unavoidable part of it, and letting it show on my face would just worry people, right?"

No matter how she raged against it, it was a set fact of life that she would periodically be visited by this poor condition, and she had accepted it as inevitable.

She had also grown accustomed to the pain it brought, so when there were other people around, she tried her best not to let it show in her expressions and movements. But since Amane had put two and two together, there wasn't much point.

Though she wanted to avoid making Amane worry, she was also happy he was concerned for her, and she enjoyed having him look after her like this. Holding these contradictory sentiments, Mahiru looked over at Amane beside her, and she saw he was staring at her with a deadly serious expression.

"I mean, how could you not worry over someone who was feeling bad? My mom's were real heavy, so I heard all about it… If there's anything I can do, I will, of course."

At times like this, the quality of Amane's upbringing, or maybe his essential good nature, was really striking.

The fact that Amane's parents had given him an outstanding education had really become clear to her over the half year she'd spent close to him.

Though he could be a little sarcastic sometimes, he was honest and flexible, and he paid close attention to others. He was capable of casually offering whatever assistance was needed, and he did so without expecting anything in return. He looked after her as if it was the obvious thing to do, and he treated her like she was important.

He lacked self-confidence, so he tended to be careless about his own well-being, and that was a flaw, but he had plenty of strong points to make up for that.

That carelessness of his had been improving lately, but even when it got bad, he was such a wonderful person in Mahiru's eyes it made her inclined to let him off easy.

"That is just what you would say, Amane."

"Sure, anyone would… You too. When I wasn't feeling well, you forced me to go to bed, didn't you?"

"Well, that was—"

"Didn't you?"

Against her better judgment, she laughed at Amane, who had puffed up his chest, brimming with confidence for some reason. That sent a shock of pain through her belly, causing her to stiffen for a moment. As soon as he saw that, Amane got a disheartened, concerned, and somewhat uneasy look in his eye, and he cast a worried glance at Mahiru.

"Um, if you're feeling really bad, I think it might be better for you to go home. You should lie down in peace and quiet. But then again, maybe it's not so painful that you can't stand it, huh? ...I know when you're not feeling well, sometimes people are a nuisance, but sometimes you feel lonely without anyone around, so I think you should be wherever you decide is best, Mahiru."

As Amane mumbled this explanation, obviously flustered and embarrassed, Mahiru covered her mouth and smiled.

She was really no match for her boyfriend, who had made this suggestion that was so thoroughly caring and kind.

"...For now, I'd rather be here, with you."

At the moment, she felt like sitting back and being pampered.

Rightfully, she should have hurried off home so she didn't inconvenience him, and if she was the same person she'd been when she'd first met him, she probably would have made up some excuse and gone home. But today's Mahiru could depend on Amane.

That was how deeply Amane's presence had entered into the soft places inside her, and the thought filled her with warmth and gave her a strange tickling feeling deep within her heart.

"...It's not incredibly painful or anything. It just makes doing things uncomfortable; that's all."

"Right. Tonight I'm making dinner."

"...You are?"

"Leave it to me. I've got an outstanding teacher, so even I can make a little something nowadays."

"Heh-heh, my student's been pretty outstanding, too, you know?"

"You're really good at teaching, Mahiru."

Though Amane said that, the fact was that most of his improvement was because of how quickly he comprehended things.

When they'd first met, he had been a terrible cook, making things like burned vegetable stir fry and ragged, overcooked omelets, but once she'd shown him some examples and taught him the rationale behind how things were cooked, he had absorbed it all immediately.

Amane had always been the type who could sit down and study, so once he'd realized cooking was akin to chemistry, he had very quickly picked up different cooking techniques.

His skills were still a little unpolished, but Amane had made food for them before, and he was refining his techniques by assisting her every day.

And so she wasn't worried about the idea of Amane cooking.

"Anything you feel like eating?"

"…I don't have any really strong cravings, so long as it's warm and not too spicy…"

"Got it. I'll do my best with what we have in the fridge."

"You've grown so much."

"See, I am capable of learning."

"Heh-heh."

Just lightly chatting like this seemed to ease the fatigue in her body.

It also seemed like Amane was deliberately talking in a slightly more cheerful tone of voice, to distract Mahiru. Actually, she mused, while they were talking like this, she felt pretty good.

"…Did you take some medicine?"

"Yes."

"Okay. Anything else you want me to do?"

Mahiru hesitated, afraid she might completely take advantage of Amane since he'd asked so affectionately, but Amane whispered to her devilishly, "You can take advantage of me as much as you like," so after a little groan, Mahiru glanced over at him.

"I'd like to nap, just a little. But I don't want to…go home."

Still, it would be wrong for her to borrow his bed, so she meant that she wanted to snooze on the sofa for a while, but Amane blinked his eyes in surprise.

She might have expected a jab about her wanting to sleep at a guy's place, but frankly she had dozed off at Amane's apartment many times before, and after all, she had full faith that Amane wouldn't try anything with a person who was feeling unwell, so that's why she had asked.

When she looked at him nervously, wondering if she had made him uncomfortable, Amane wore an awkward smile that was more bashful than it was uncomfortable.

Gently, he placed his large palm on top of her head.

"It's fine. Take it easy and rest. I'm right here with you."

"…Okay."

Mahiru slowly closed her eyes, basking in the soft, warm tones of his voice, which seemed to wrap her up, and she leaned against Amane's arm.

She felt an exaggerated shiver of surprise for a moment, but Mahiru didn't feel like pulling away.

He said he'd be by my side, after all.

In which case, leaning on him like that should have been just fine.

The heat that gradually spread to her from their point of contact felt pleasant.

When she turned her face toward Amane a little bit, his refreshing and now-familiar minty smell, as well as the faint aroma of fabric softener, tickled her nasal cavity.

Her face curved into a smile at the mellow, calming scents, and Mahiru let go of consciousness right there, while enjoying his pleasant warmth.

When she awoke from a dream that was full of warmth, Mahiru slowly opened her eyes. As she lifted the curtain of sleep from her eyes, she saw that her view was filled with gray.

Her mind, which was working considerably more slowly than

usual, thought back dimly to what she had just been doing. Though she remembered after a moment that she had taken a nap, she lifted her head sluggishly, not processing what she was seeing.

A twinkle of obsidian entered her field of vision.

"Morning."

In response to the person who had whispered to her in a soft, mellow voice, Mahiru stiffened for a moment in confusion.

Amane, the owner of the voice, continued in a gentle tone, as if to urge her to fully wake up, "Did you sleep well?"

"……Good morning."

At that point, Mahiru remembered the crucial piece of information, that she had fallen asleep leaning against Amane, and without meaning to, she answered him in a shrill voice.

She'd thought she was awfully warm and comfortable, and if she had been dozing away without a care while feeling Amane's body heat, then of course she was warm.

Though her body felt a little bit stiff, mentally, on the other hand, she felt so completely content that she had no complaints.

"Ah, let me just say this, this is, well, it was your doing, so…and I felt bad shaking you off."

"This…?"

As Mahiru puzzled over what Amane had told her, and the worried look on his face, she identified the "this" Amane had indicated, then buried her face in his upper arm once more.

Without noticing it, she had grabbed ahold of Amane's hand tightly and intertwined their fingers. Almost as if she was trying to tell him not to let go, as if to stop his clumsy fingers from leaving, she had slipped her own fingers between them.

Once he pointed out that she had apparently not been satisfied just leaning against him, and had grabbed his hand as well, Mahiru couldn't do anything but try not to groan.

The way she was sitting, she had definitely prevented Amane from moving. After leaning against him, she had completely stolen the freedom of one of his hands, which must have been troublesome for Amane.

"S-sorry, I was in your way, huh?"

"Not at all, but…I wonder if you were having a bit of a hard time sleeping? Though it seems a bit late to say that, after you fell asleep sitting up."

"N-no, I was fast asleep!"

When she tried to dismiss the idea with a wave of her hand, she realized their hands were still connected, and she quickly let go. Amane must have found Mahiru's panic amusing, because he made a low noise in his throat as he laughed and, without pausing, used careful movements to gently untangle their intertwined fingers.

Resisting the urge to cry out as she was for some reason beset by a sudden feeling of loss, Mahiru realized she couldn't keep leaning against him forever, and she sat back up on the sofa. Then she looked up at Amane, who appeared to have straightened up as well.

Being who he was, Amane seemed to be able to tell Mahiru was acting livelier than she had before her nap, and he was looking at her with relief in his eyes.

"Is your medicine working?"

"Yes. And I feel much better. Sorry for the bother."

Just as she had said, she felt like she had really inconvenienced him.

She'd made him worry about her, and then she had substantially restricted his movements. She was sure Amane must have been really bored, stuck to the sofa like that.

Plus, since she had been leaning against him, she'd put some part of her body weight on him, which must have worn him out for no good reason.

She felt really guilty about all of that, but Amane blinked his black eyes several times without changing his usual expression. He looked like he didn't understand why he had been apologized to.

"Why are you apologizing? It was no bother; in fact, I'm glad you let me help."

"...Please don't spoil me like that."

"You're one to talk, when you're always spoiling me!"

Amane squished her cheeks and insisted she let him spoil her, too, and the ticklish feeling made her narrow her eyes at him.

"That's one thing; this is another."

"What a sneaky trick."

"Heh-heh, I'm a sneaky girl."

If she made too big a fuss, Amane would worry, so when she showed him this defiant attitude, while also feeling grateful for his gentlemanly kindness, Amane put on an openly displeased look, and she laughed in spite of herself.

She couldn't tell whether it was thanks to taking a little nap and laughing together like this, or whether it was simply thanks to the medication, but although she was a little bit stiff, her body felt much lighter than before.

She glanced over at the clock and saw that she had apparently slept for a little less than an hour.

Under normal circumstances, it wouldn't have been strange for her to have finished making dinner by this time. Feeling guilty that she had inconvenienced Amane, she started to stand up, saying, "I'll get dinner ready," and she found that she couldn't stand.

It wasn't because her body felt too heavy.

It was because Amane was physically holding her down.

To be more accurate, he was restraining her with his arm, keeping Mahiru from moving, and though he was using a gentle level of force, his gesture was full of determination to absolutely not allow her to stand.

"You sit down, Mahiru."

"Huh, but I feel better—"

"But you're not back to normal, are you? You still seem a little sluggish. Come on, I promised I would make dinner, so let me keep my promise, okay?"

Though Amane had indeed said he would make dinner, since she was recovered to the point that she could pretty much move normally, she wanted to protest. But when she looked at Amane's eyes, she could tell he was absolutely not going to back down.

This was another thing she had learned since getting close to him. Although Amane was basically a pushover, once he decided to do something, there was no stopping him.

When he got like this, resistance was futile, and he wouldn't give up until she folded.

The reason he wouldn't give up was basically because he was doing something for someone else, so Mahiru couldn't protest too much.

At the moment he was giving Mahiru a reproachful look because she was making a discontented expression at him. But the look in his eyes was powerful, and she could see he wasn't going to give in, even though he was wearing a wry smile.

"Don't sulk like that… Quit trying to do things on your own. Lean on me."

"…Fine."

"Great. Just stay here; you're in good hands… Though they might be rough compared to yours."

"Geez."

Mahiru smiled at his self-deprecating answer, and Amane smiled similarly and ruffled her hair.

She knew this stroke of her head was meant to reassure her, so she calmly, happily accepted it.

She was convinced it was a special gesture, something he did only to her.

"...It's gonna take me a little while, so you can sleep a little bit more if you want to."

"That's okay. I'll watch you heroically working away from here."

"You're such a worrier."

Smiling in amusement, Amane headed for the kitchen, and Mahiru watched him go, filled with euphoria and a sense of security.

She wasn't watching him out of concern, but because she was incredibly, unbearably happy he was trying so hard for her sake, and because she wanted to watch carefully so she didn't miss any of those sentiments in action. She doubted Amane was aware of it as she watched him work.

She couldn't help but find it charming as he put on the simple apron he used.

Just like a little family.

Holding on to this fantasy, Mahiru kept Amane firmly in her sights as he began to grapple with the dinner ingredients.

Less than an hour had gone by before there was a plate in front of Mahiru's eyes, letting off steam along with a fragrant aroma.

Even though she was just going from the sofa to the dining table, she got a courteous escort for the move. Mahiru blinked several times at the dish Amane had made.

When she'd asked for something warm and not too spicy, she had expected to get something in the realm of porridge. Amane had definitely used rice, but this was something completely different.

Served up in deep dishes, it was a cream-colored risotto, and she could tell it was thick. Based on the smell and the appearance, she figured it was indeed a creamy risotto. It wasn't just rice; it had a little bit of mushrooms and spinach added in, which gave it accents of dark reddish brown and green as well.

"It's a soy-milk risotto, but, uh, I went ahead and made it from uncooked rice. I also used the mushrooms and spinach that were in the fridge. I hope that's okay?"

Mahiru was taken aback by this explanation, which really made her aware of Amane's growth, and Amane added, with definite confidence, "I told you I was going to make you a proper dinner."

It wasn't like she hadn't believed him, but she hadn't expected Amane's culinary repertoire to include something like this, so it was way beyond her expectations, and she froze up.

"Those ingredients sound fine. It looks delicious."

"I'm glad. I don't know what I would do if you said you didn't want it."

"Amane, you know I'm not picky about food."

"Well sure, that's true, but still…I was worried it might not be what you were in the mood for."

"There's no way I could possibly complain when I gave you such a vague order and left it all up to you to make dinner for me…"

Though she was delighted enough just by his determination, he had also really prepared something, and what's more, with the dish he had made, he had shown her the results of all the hard work she'd seen him put in, starting at a time when it would have been accurate to say he pretty much couldn't cook at all.

"It was really clever of you to make risotto."

"I didn't necessarily make it because I thought you had no appetite. I just did a little looking online and decided on this. Instead of consommé, I tried putting *shirodashi* and miso paste in it. It seems like that would give it more of a comforting flavor. I gave it a taste, and I don't think there's anything wrong with it, but…"

"This changes my whole concept of what you're capable of…"

"I'm not sure how I feel about you being that impressed, but even I can manage if I put my mind to it!"

Looking a little conflicted over how Mahiru had frozen, Amane brought her a spoon, and Mahiru smiled and accepted it.

"Thank you very much," she said, and then looked at the freshly made risotto again. "Can I start eating?"

"Sure, go ahead."

Mahiru smiled at Amane, who looked a little nervous as he watched her. Then she mumbled a few words of thanks for the meal, and scooped up some risotto with her spoon.

She knew it had just been made and it was still quite hot, so she blew on it to cool it off a little before bringing it to her mouth. Simmered dishes like this capitalized on the richness of the sauce and the firmness of the rice.

Maybe because it was made from uncooked rice, it was smoother than it looked, but not too thick, and it melted perfectly in her mouth.

The moment the risotto began to dissolve in her mouth, it produced a tender kind of flavor consisting of lightly fragrant butter and mellow soy milk, underneath which the *shirodashi* was low-key but certainly present at the center of everything.

Amane had said he'd used miso, and she figured it was thanks to the miso that the risotto was so light but with a definite richness to it. It barely asserted its existence and wasn't that detectable, but it inconspicuously added depth to the flavor. He really ought to have said it was a secret ingredient.

The mushrooms, which were cut a little on the small side, had also blended into the risotto, adding umami, so on the whole, the dish had a mild and subdued yet deeply nourishing and comforting flavor.

"...How is it?"

"It's delicious."

"And what percent of that is flattery?"

"Don't just assume I'm flattering you, geez."

Certainly, the delicious flavor had made her pause, but it wasn't like she was taking time to come up with some flattering answer to give him.

She complained to Amane, with a look that said they didn't have the type of relationship where they needed to flatter each other, and he answered her with a slightly apologetic look.

"It's good, like properly good. I can tell you were careful when you were making it. It's got a gentle flavor that makes good use of the ingredients."

"I'm glad to hear that. Now I can eat, too."

Amane seemed embarrassed by Mahiru's honest praise. He gave thanks for the food and raised a bite of risotto to his mouth.

It sounded like he had tested it already, so he probably knew what it tasted like, and he wasn't as excited about it as Mahiru, but he did narrow his eyes and look fairly satisfied.

"It's good, but it still has a long way to go before it can compare to something you made, Mahiru."

"Why do you have to compare them like that? Actually, I think you must be incredibly talented to catch up to me so quickly, when I've been cooking for ten or so years already."

"In that case, I'll never catch up, not in my whole life."

Though he had developed quickly, Amane was nowhere close to catching up to Mahiru in terms of her skills, experience, and knowledge about cooking. Actually, she thought she would be pretty embarrassed if he had caught up to her. But no matter how good he got, it wouldn't change anything about them cooking together, and once Mahiru arrived at that thought, she felt ashamed by how narrow-minded she was for wishing he would always need to rely on her just a little.

"But it is tasty, really… The flavor warms you up. Comforting, I guess I could call it. It's got your kindness blended right in, Amane."

"I never knew kindness was a flavor."

"Your palate is influenced by your intentions, so putting your sincerity into your cooking also increases how delicious it is."

Not everything in cooking was necessarily determined just by skill.

Of course, it went without saying that the flavor of one's cooking was determined by the skills of the chef, but the creator's intentions also played a part in the finished dish.

Mahiru thought her dinner tasted even better because she knew the effort and thoughtfulness of the cook.

"...Plus, there's also the simple fact you've gotten better at cooking, Amane. The firmness of the rice is just right, and the flavor is delicate and unified."

"I'm honored by your kind words."

"...Are you making fun of me?"

"I'm not making fun... No, really, I'm grateful."

"I'm the one who should be grateful over here, geez."

He had realized right away she wasn't feeling well. Then he looked after her, let her lean against him, and even made her dinner. Amane was so kind and considerate, pampering her like this.

What more could she possibly want? She felt so grateful toward him, after all he had done for her.

Amane probably didn't have a good sense of this, but his major strong point was his ability to be kind to others and to get things done with such composure, as if they were no big deal, even if they were.

Amane was obviously still concerned Mahiru was suffering. She looked at him and quietly mumbled, "That's so like you," then went back to her spoon.

The two of them finished eating and took a small break, before Amane started preparing to clean up.

Mahiru looked up at him. "Next time, I'll try not to place this kind of burden on you."

This time, she'd had Amane looking after her, and although that had made things easy on her, it had placed the burden on only one of them, since he had made dinner for them both. She didn't think that was a good thing, and that's why she had made that remark.

But Amane said curiously, "Why?" and it was Mahiru's turn to look surprised.

"Huh, what do you mean, why? It was a lot of work for you, right?"

"No? Why?"

Amane looked a little extra young and cute as he stared at her blankly, but the words he said next were a strong demonstration of how dependable he was.

"If anything, I wish you'd depend on me more. Trying to push through when you're not feeling well is just going to make you feel worse for longer. It's actually better for me, too, if you rest."

"B-but then—"

"And anyway, this is not really much of a burden."

He seemed a little dissatisfied with the suggestion that she couldn't rely on him, and Mahiru, unable to look directly at him, cast her eyes downward.

"…If you say things like that, I'm going to get carried away and depend on you for everything."

"Go ahead, leave lots of stuff up to me. Now, not to be pushy, but please, sit down. I'll come in after I wash the dishes. Let me handle it. Go on."

"…Okay."

Amane smiled, as if he didn't consider it much of a burden at all. He patted her head, saying, "Mm, good," and she found herself staring vacantly at him.

I love him so much.

He was a kind, dependable person, who was good at looking after others and never spared any effort.

Amane's kindness in phrasing it that way, to get Mahiru to rely on him without fretting about it, was something that took her a moment to grasp fully.

Amane had said what he said because he knew Mahiru could never just passively depend on him. It showed he had a deep understanding of how she operated.

A person like him would make an ideal husband, she found herself fantasizing.

Mahiru was completely enchanted by Amane's mature-looking smile, but his eyebrows knit together, and he frowned.

"...You must really be feeling pretty bad, huh? Do you want to go home early and sleep?"

In his mind, Amane must have connected Mahiru making a spaced-out expression with her feeling bad. Mahiru panicked and shook her head, sorry she had caused him needless worry.

"N-no that's not—! You...p-promise you won't laugh?"

"What is it?"

"...I was thinking about what a good husband you'll make."

Mahiru felt embarrassed for saying something so crazy and out of character, but Amane didn't recoil; he just exuded surprise and a little bit of awkwardness.

"Th-there wasn't any deeper meaning behind it, okay?! It's just, that's how I felt with you taking care of me like this, and taking the initiative, and looking after me; that's what I was thinking about."

The fact that everything she said sounded like an excuse was probably because she was self-conscious about her own feelings. Her attempts to keep her overwhelming feelings of love for Amane in check weren't working, and she'd blurted out outrageous things without really thinking them through. It made her keenly aware that her emotions were indeed unstable during this time of the month.

Though she tried to somehow keep control over her cheeks as

they began to heat up on their own, just thinking about being under Amane's gaze seemed to add fuel to the fire of her happiness and embarrassment, and her face blazed brightly.

Unable to stand it, she made what was probably one of the top three most pitiful noises of her life and hung her head. "Ahhhhh."

Amane looked majorly dismayed again. "I-I'm happy to have you thinking something like that, then. But…something like this is just normal, right? Go on, rest now, rest."

Speaking very quickly and in clipped tones, Amane quite nimbly set all the dishes on a tray and escaped into the kitchen.

Mahiru couldn't bring herself to lift her head; all she could do was curl up into a ball and stare at the floor.

Her physical pain had completely disappeared, and in its place, the warm glow that had always been there had transformed into a blaze that just wouldn't burn out. She was going to require quite a bit of time to suppress that burning passion.

The Future We're Walking Into

The first time Mahiru was ever faced with clear hostility was around the time she turned ten years old.

"Miss Shiina, you're a sneaky one."

On the way home from school one time, she found herself alone with another classmate, who suddenly said that.

Normally, she went home with one of her friends, but on that day, her friend had plans with someone else. And so, since they were headed in the same direction, Mahiru just happened to walk home with another girl in her class, someone she didn't know very well.

Generally speaking, Mahiru got along fairly well with everybody, and as they made their way home, the two of them had been chatting casually, having a harmless conversation, so the girl's remark seemed to come out of nowhere.

"Sneaky? I am? How?"

Since she hadn't initially said what specifically was sneaky, Mahiru couldn't even begin to guess, and she waited with a questioning look for the girl to continue. The girl must have taken that for a look of calm and glared sharply back at her.

Normally, the other girl was quite mild-mannered, so it was

completely unexpected to face this level of animosity from her, and Mahiru couldn't help but feel bewildered.

After all, Mahiru always behaved herself at school, or at least that's how she perceived her actions. She never excluded anybody, and she acted in a friendly way without ever letting the smile fade from her face.

Her behavior didn't change, even toward this girl who rarely talked to her. If anything, she had sometimes looked out for this girl, who tended to be excluded from things, and Mahiru did her best to make sure she wouldn't be ostracized.

If the girl disliked that, then Mahiru could understand her being angry, but the word she had used was *sneaky*, and it didn't seem like she had any bad feelings about how Mahiru handled things at school.

Mahiru really didn't have any clue what the girl was talking about, so the only answer she could give was that she didn't understand. The girl seemed infuriated by that reply and dramatically frowned as she said with a trembling lip, "Suzuki's in love with you!"

Her tone of voice was extremely sharp, and she was definitely sulking. But at least Mahiru understood why she was so upset.

However, Mahiru still didn't understand why that made her sneaky.

The Suzuki that the girl was talking about was one of their male classmates. He had recently started talking to Mahiru. That had to be the Suzuki that the other girl was talking about.

Certainly, Suzuki had approached her, and even asked her out, but as far as Mahiru was concerned, that was all that had happened. But the other girl's anger seemed to escalate even more when Mahiru did not show much of a reaction.

"He's always talking to you, and inviting you to hang out with him, and smiling at you, isn't he?!"

The reason he had come to speak to her was because he was at the

©Hanekoto

center of a group of popular boys, and Mahiru, being Mahiru, was at the center of a group of popular girls. So they'd happened to have the opportunity to talk; that was all.

It was true he had paid some attention to her, but Suzuki was the type who was always smiling, so it wasn't inaccurate to say he had been smiling at Mahiru. But for Mahiru, who always treated everyone the same, the only reaction she could have to being attacked like this was confusion.

"I liked Suzuki first! Can't you keep your hands off him?!"

"I don't remember ever putting any on him."

She wanted to add something about the boy not belonging to this girl in the first place, but she could tell that she wasn't in the listening mood, so she settled for a shorter answer.

"Well then, why do you talk to him? If you don't like him, knock it off!"

"But I've never talked to him as anything more than a classmate."

"Liar!"

Far from lying, Mahiru was telling the truth. But from the other girl's perspective, it didn't seem to look that way.

Mahiru was really at a loss for how to explain things so the other girl would understand.

To Mahiru, Suzuki was simply a classmate, and she didn't have even the slightest interest in him as a member of the opposite sex. If anything, he wasn't her type.

Though she acted like a good girl and played the part of someone who was cheerful and sociable, the real Mahiru was the type of girl who wanted to live quietly and not be disturbed by others as she lived her life.

The boy was cheerful and friendly, and so naturally he got along well with people.

But Mahiru didn't care for the way he approached her and talked to her as if they had been good friends for a long time, even though they didn't know each other that well. She didn't like the type of people who came on so strongly without realizing how the other party might feel about it.

Upon reflection, Mahiru concluded that it was possible that because Suzuki was pushy and overly familiar with everyone and Mahiru treated everyone the same, the girl had gotten the wrong idea. She felt a little bad.

But still, Mahiru was certain she hadn't acted as if she liked Suzuki, even a little bit, so she couldn't help but be a bit annoyed by the accusation.

"Anyway, don't get too friendly with Suzuki."

"Sure, if that's what you want, Miss Inoue."

For some reason, Mahiru was getting ordered around. But she didn't particularly want to talk to Suzuki anyway, and she was happy keeping the same comfortable distance with him as with any other classmate, so the demand didn't bother her at all, and she accepted it easily.

The other girl seemed satisfied with that, and she snorted and pushed her way past Mahiru to leave, bumping into her as she went as if to say that she had no more business with her.

Mahiru stood there flabbergasted, watching the other girl's back as she ran off, her backpack swaying. "That was awful," she muttered.

Mahiru hadn't really had much to do with Inoue before but had always thought she was quiet and well-behaved. She was surprised to find this girl apparently had a nasty temper.

Reevaluating her opinions after this unexpected exchange, Mahiru followed the road home, walking the same way she always did.

"Young lady, you should know that girls can get aggressive when it seems like the person they care for might be taken from them. Especially when they are young."

Mahiru had never been in love and didn't really understand the other girl's feelings. Miss Koyuki had come to do the housework, and when Mahiru talked to her about the incident after school, she gave her this answer gently, with a strained smile.

Miss Koyuki's way of gently, gently warning Mahiru, which was not at all a rebuke, only made things even less clear.

She just couldn't understand why someone would become aggressive when they fell in love. She could only wonder how someone could take that out on others.

"He might be taken? But I don't even want him!"

"That's awfully harsh, young lady."

She looked at Miss Koyuki and insisted that it couldn't be helped, since she really didn't want the boy, but Miss Koyuki kept wearing the same strained smile.

"Well, when you're in love with someone, you get scared that the person you care for might become someone else's sweetheart. You worry greatly that the one you want might be taken from you, right out from under your nose, and you may end up confronting the person who seems likely to steal them, asking them to back down."

"So she's warning me off?"

"I believe so, yes."

In that case, Mahiru could appreciate the principle behind the girl's conduct, but there was something else she understood even less now.

"But Suzuki never belonged to that girl in the first place. I don't understand how she can tell me not to take him. When did she get the right to say things like that?"

The girl had spoken as if Suzuki was already completely in her possession, and Mahiru found that curious.

She felt like the girl hadn't even had that much contact with Suzuki anyway, and...though she searched through her memories, she couldn't recall her ever approaching Suzuki before. She had seen her timidly speak to him, but that was all.

"Not everyone is able to separate facts from their feelings as well as you can, young lady. I'm sure that someday you, too, will understand her state of mind, so we mustn't speak badly about the girl. Besides, you will antagonize her if you say you don't care for the boy, so how about you keep that to yourself, all right?"

"What for?"

"Hearing someone say they don't care about something you want can make you feel like they are mocking you or questioning why you want that thing."

"So even though she's the one who told me not to take him, if I say I don't want him, she'll get angry? That's so strange."

"Humans can be that way."

Miss Koyuki had vastly more life experience than Mahiru, so if she said that was so, Mahiru was satisfied that it was. But still, she felt a surge of feeling like she didn't want anything to do with people who brandished their emotions like blunt weapons.

"Knowing you don't want to take the boy and throwing that fact in the other girl's face are two different things. You understand that, don't you, young lady?"

"Yes."

"Very good… I think you will understand once there is someone you like. I think you will understand the anxiety that comes when the person you like looks at another girl."

"…Someone I like?"

Even hearing it from Miss Koyuki, the idea didn't quite sit right with Mahiru.

Among Mahiru's few personal relationships, Miss Koyuki was the person she liked the best, but of course, she didn't have feelings of romantic love toward her, nor could she imagine having any feelings for a boy that surpassed what she felt for Miss Koyuki.

She had often seen books that said girls developed mentally earlier than boys, and honestly, it did seem to Mahiru that the boys in her class were more childish. That didn't necessarily mean she looked down on them, but they did a lot of impulsive, impetuous things, and interacting with them tired her out.

Mahiru had always been aware that she was also too mature for her age, and she had had the sense that she was never able to get very close to her peers because there was too much of a gap between them. They weren't on the same wavelength, she could say.

Because of that, she had never been able to clearly imagine herself falling in love with someone. But she knew that it would probably happen once she was grown up, so she intended to take Miss Koyuki's warnings seriously.

"Even if I do start liking somebody, I don't want to take it out on anyone else."

"That's right. Plus, if the person you like hears other people complain about you, that will make it more difficult for you to get close to that person."

"Difficult?"

"Suppose there was someone who liked you, young lady, and that person forcefully confronted your good friends with their selfish feelings; what would you think of that?"

"I would stay away from that person."

Mahiru understood that it was obviously best not to become too friendly with that type of person.

"Exactly. You would be afraid of them, right?"

"Yes."

If someone was careless with things others valued, she really doubted they would treat her with any more care.

She could imagine such a person would force their ideas of what was important onto her, and she would get hurt, so Mahiru wasn't interested in getting close to anyone like that.

Once she considered that, leaving aside the question of whether Suzuki actually liked Mahiru, the kind of girl who would aggressively confront anyone she even suspected he liked was obviously a hurtful person.

She understood why Inoue had gotten aggressive and jealous and called her sneaky, and Mahiru wasn't angry about it, but she also thought the girl could have found a better way to address her feelings.

"But what I'm curious about is why did she just call me sneaky, rather than trying to get the person she likes to like her back? Does she think she can get him to like her just by calling me names?"

If the girl thought Mahiru was so sneaky, perhaps she ought to become more like Mahiru. Shouldn't she, Mahiru wondered, make some effort to get the boy to turn and look at her?

She wasn't saying the girl hadn't made any effort, but as far as Mahiru had seen, she'd hardly done anything to appeal to the boy and get him to like her. She never proactively went to talk to him, and she didn't seem to be trying to learn about the things he liked.

Even Mahiru, who didn't understand anything about love, thought it would be difficult to get someone to love you that way.

"Hmm. Young lady, you mustn't ask that question of anyone else, all right?"

"Okay. I only said it because I'm asking you, Miss Koyuki."

Even Mahiru, in the short amount of time she had lived, had determined there were certain social boundaries that had to be observed and that other people would reject her if she said certain things out loud. In order to be a good girl, she had been trying the best she could not to get on people's nerves.

Mahiru knew it wouldn't be wise to ask the other girl whatever came to mind. But "why" was the only question Mahiru hadn't been able to resolve on her own, so she had asked Miss Koyuki, who was an adult and someone she trusted.

To Mahiru, trying hard was normal, and although it was often difficult, Mahiru was never opposed to putting in the necessary effort.

She had always thought if someone did their best, so long as there were no adverse conditions, they would be able to accomplish their desired goal.

That was exactly what made this so curious.

Still, leaving aside the question of whether or not the girl could even possess the boy in the first place, since it was a matter of human relations after all, if she never gave it any effort, she wouldn't even be able to get him to look her way. So why was she failing to put any effort in? Mahiru wondered.

Could she get the boy just by saying she wanted him?

Despite not making any effort at all, this girl was already getting the kind of love Mahiru desperately wanted and worked so hard for, yet could never have. Why did she think she could get even more love just by wanting it and not putting in any work?

That was what Mahiru wondered, just a little.

Miss Koyuki smiled calmly, and it was unclear whether or not she was aware of the complicated mix of feelings in Mahiru's heart, but she gently bent forward so she could meet Mahiru's gaze, and she peered into her face.

"Young lady, you try hard at everything you do, so I suppose you might not understand it."

Even Mahiru could tell there was something bitter, like faint pity, in Miss Koyuki's voice.

"There are many fewer people than you think who are willing to work hard for what they desire, no matter how difficult it might be, without knowing whether or not their wish will be granted. Your ability to keep on trying is another way in which you are gifted."

"...Gifted?"

"People like to take the easy way out and believe that great things will just fall into their laps without them having to lift a finger... They tend to take the path of least resistance."

"Do things ever work out that way?"

"Mm, good question. Sometimes good things do happen, so I suppose it is possible. The question is what you do from there. People convince themselves a bit of good luck from out of nowhere is going to continue forever. Things worked out one way before, so they ought to work out a certain way next time, they think... And as a result of chasing that one-time bout of good luck, and ceasing to make any effort of their own, it's possible that people get nothing and waste their time and never manage to acquire the things they want."

What Miss Koyuki was saying reminded Mahiru of a nursery rhyme she had heard somewhere before. She wasn't sure why, but it sounded like Miss Koyuki's warning was accompanied by real-life experience.

Mahiru quietly listened to her words, which were gently spoken but had the edge of a moral lesson. Miss Koyuki smiled sweetly at her.

"I got a little off track, but the point is that you, young lady, are diligent and hardworking. I think that those are wonderful qualities and strong points you ought to be proud of."

Adding that Mahiru mustn't demand the same level of effort from others, Miss Koyuki squeezed her hand.

Although Mahiru was growing up, an adult's hand still seemed big to her, the way it completely enveloped her own.

She didn't dislike it—in fact, it made her happy, which must have been because, in a very real sense, Mahiru couldn't get anyone else to reach out for her hand. Miss Koyuki was the only one who knew

Mahiru's exact feelings and the only person who could touch Mahiru without making her uncomfortable.

"Young lady, once you've found someone you love, you must do everything you can to get them to look your way... I think that anyone who measures up to your standards will probably be someone truly amazing. When you've got something good, other people are always after it. If you don't hold on tight with your own two hands, it might slip right through your fingers. That's the last thing you'd want to happen, right?"

"...Yes."

Though she nodded in agreement, Mahiru couldn't quite picture it.

She just couldn't imagine having someone she loved by her side.

Actually, since she had never had someone snuggle up to her before, it was more accurate to say she didn't even know what that would look like.

"But you're talking about what happens when I find someone I love. I don't even want to do that."

"What would your ideal partner be like, young lady?"

"...Someone who would make a family with me."

Miss Koyuki's face clouded over at the words that rushed from Mahiru's mouth, and Mahiru immediately regretted saying them.

Miss Koyuki was the person most bothered by Mahiru's relationship with her parents, other than Mahiru, and the word *family* always put her on edge.

She knew Mahiru had already mostly given up. No matter how much Mahiru wanted it, even if she screamed and cried until she ran out of tears, her two parents would never look her way.

That was all the more reason why maybe, just maybe—if Mahiru ever fell for someone else, she hoped it would be someone who would snuggle up close to her, someone with whom she could pass the days as a family.

"If you make a connection with a wonderful person, then in the end, you'll be able to build a family. Before that, while you're dating, is there anything you think you will look for?"

"...I'd like someone who listens carefully to what I say, someone who will stay by my side and who makes me feel relaxed when I'm with them. Someone who will think things over with me when I don't understand them and stay with me patiently when things get tough. That would be good."

Mahiru couldn't imagine ever falling in love with a boy.

But if she did, she was sure it would be someone like that.

Someone who would listen carefully to her, who would stay by her side, who would have eyes only for her, and who would treasure her always.

...I wonder if anyone will ever love me?

Mahiru had always felt like she was not really an attractive person.

She could tell people liked her good-girl persona, but she couldn't imagine anyone would ever like the real her once that facade was stripped away.

And anyway, at the moment, there was nothing to indicate that she was ever going to fall for someone, so it still didn't feel like something that could really happen.

Mahiru thought it was probably all right to just hold on to the fleeting wish that it might be nice to have someone someday. When she looked up at Miss Koyuki, who was holding her hand, Miss Koyuki squeezed her hand a little more firmly.

"I'm sure you will also meet a good person someday, young lady."

"...Right."

"You mustn't get mixed up with worthless men. Anyone who sees you as something to be consumed, or who doesn't see you as his equal, or who tries to tell you what kind of person you have to be is no good. Find yourself someone who will see you for who you are, who will see the effort you put in and recognize your worth, someone who will accept you as you are, who is honest and kind… I won't be able to stay by your side forever, young lady. There is nothing I can do but hope you will find someone who will make you happy."

When she heard those last words, added in a hoarse voice, Mahiru finally understood why Miss Koyuki was warning her so sternly about all this.

There was no way Miss Koyuki was going to be able to stay by Mahiru's side forever.

Miss Koyuki was not Mahiru's mother. She was employed as a housekeeper, and was a complete stranger otherwise. Her relationship to Mahiru was weak enough that if her parents ever fired Miss Koyuki on some kind of whim, it would sever the bond between them.

Even though she often fulfilled a maternal role, just like she was doing at the moment, Miss Koyuki never acted as if she were Mahiru's actual mother. She called Mahiru "young lady" and maintained a certain amount of distance, probably so she didn't give Mahiru any naive hopes.

That was because, no matter what happened, Miss Koyuki could not become Mahiru's mother.

Having that fact thrust at her dispassionately and yet directly, Mahiru bit her lip, and Miss Koyuki once again wrapped up Mahiru's little hand in hers.

A deeply penetrating warmth traveled through Mahiru's hand and collected near her eyes, where it warmed her whole face.

"You have to always try your best, young lady, so you can win the love of someone who will make you happy. I suspect all sorts of different people will probably approach you. There may be people who want to use you and people who will speak ill of you. However, they will never be able to diminish or take away the time and effort you put into yourself… I'm certain someone will come along who loves you for exactly who you are and not just for your appearance or your abilities."

She wasn't Mahiru's mother, but Miss Koyuki was the person most concerned about Mahiru and most worried about her future prospects. And she was the only one who told her things in an attempt to gently guide her toward a brighter future. Mahiru felt a sensation like something tightening in her chest as she gave a small nod, then hung her head.

"So I guess that's why I haven't gotten mixed up with any bad men."

Mahiru had been staring down at the pages, which were a little yellowed and faded. One way or another, she thought, Miss Koyuki's instructions had been correct, and Mahiru's heart had not steered her off course. With a rustle of pages, she closed the diary shut.

It made a snapping noise as the air was pushed out and the pages collided, but Mahiru paid no attention to that. She half rose as she closed the notebook, then returned to her seat again after setting it on the table in front of her.

Without any hesitation, she leaned her whole body back and bent her neck to look upward, where she locked eyes with Amane, on whom she was lying instead of the sofa.

Mahiru had gotten quite used to sitting in between Amane's legs, and even though she still felt a little shy about it, she was now able to glue herself to his side rather than sitting beside him normally. She felt happy inside as she used Amane for a chair, but he frowned slightly.

They'd been pressed right against one another until a moment earlier, so she didn't think he would have any complaints about the position, but maybe something had happened… When she gazed into his eyes, he grumbled gloomily, "Why do I feel like I'm being put down?"

That was when she realized he had misunderstood the comment she had just made to herself, and in a panic, she shook her head at Amane, who was wondering whether he should embrace her or not.

"No, no, you've got it all wrong. I was looking at my diary, and I remembered Miss Koyuki saying I mustn't get involved with any bad men."

Until a moment earlier, Mahiru had been sitting between Amane's legs, rereading her diary.

From where he was sitting, Amane had plenty of opportunities to see the contents of the diary, but perhaps out of consideration for her privacy, he hadn't even tried to peek at it. Despite that, Mahiru had been describing the sort of things that were in there as she read through the diary.

They had been laughing together, reminiscing over things that had happened to them both. But Mahiru had figured, naturally enough, that Amane wouldn't have anything to say about things that had happened in her early childhood, so while she was looking over entries from that period of her life, she had been reading silently to herself.

Because of that, it seemed like he had misunderstood the comment she'd thoughtlessly made to herself, taking it as a snide remark against him.

"What was that all about? You suddenly sounded like you were implying something."

"I'm sorry for giving you the wrong idea. I was reminiscing, and it just came out…"

"Hm, it's fine, it's okay, I misunderstood all on my own, after all."

"…You are not a bad man, Amane. Of course you aren't."

"But I am totally spoiled."

"Well…"

His tone was slightly joking, so she answered him in a slightly critical tone of her own.

"You always say that about yourself, Amane, but at this point, I don't think that's accurate anymore."

"You think so?"

"It's hard to say what I would point to and claim you're spoiled. You're clever, and you can do all the housework, you're good at taking care of people, and you're a kind, honest, and gentle person. There aren't many people like you."

"Are you sure you're not putting me up on a pedestal? That's what it sounds like."

"I'm certain. Your feet are firmly on the ground."

"Then, you must be using a very good filter when you look at me."

"I am not, geez."

Mahiru was getting annoyed with Amane's refusal to accept a compliment, but at the same time, she could understand how he was feeling, so she decided to refrain from complimenting him too much, which could have come across as mockery.

Amane himself might still feel like he had a long way to go, but from Mahiru's perspective, he was good enough. If anything, he was already better than good.

In any case, he had reached the point where he could handle any kind of housework, which put him head and shoulders above the other boys his age.

Despite that, it seemed like Amane himself had yet to accept that fact, so Mahiru usually praised him for his ambition, but she wished he would develop a more accurate picture of himself.

"Amane, you're already an impressively self-reliant guy. Actually, it would be more worth my time spoiling you if you would get a little bit more useless and depraved each day."

"Stoppp it; don't go spoiling me, please! I want to spoil you instead."

"If you do that, I won't be fit to be seen by other people anymore, will I?"

"I can barely show you off as it is, though."

With a laugh, he wrapped his arms around Mahiru's midsection, and she held her tongue.

In their current position, Mahiru was sitting in between Amane's legs, leaning back against his body and relaxing. It was a lazy posture that would have been unthinkable for Mahiru to adopt outside the house, and she looked like she was demanding his attention. If any outsider had seen her, she had no doubt they would say she'd been spoiled rotten by Amane.

Amane actually seemed happy Mahiru was acting so spoiled, and he was letting her do as she pleased, and even letting her fawn all over him, so he actually seemed to welcome this situation and be enjoying himself.

"...I could get even worse."

"I'd like you to, personally. I want us to be on equal footing and respect one another, but I also want to dote on you and completely spoil you rotten."

Amane brought his lips to the back of Mahiru's head as he whispered that in a soft but penetrating voice. She would have liked to complain to somebody for making Amane into such an unwitting romantic, but Mahiru herself and Amane's parents were probably to blame for that, so she stopped thinking about it too deeply.

Now that they had been dating for several months, Mahiru could appreciate how her own actions had helped to form the way Amane doted on her, so she was in no position to criticize him. And anyway, it wasn't like she disliked Amane's behavior when he treated her tenderly and showered her with love. So although she groaned in embarrassment, she let him do as he pleased.

He was showing his love for her, and yet Amane was still naturally cautious and reserved, and he only went so far as to kiss her and gently wrap her up in his arms to hold her.

He was determined not to make her uncomfortable, so though he spoke confidently, he was often actually quite restrained.

And yet this time, he seemed to want to be really affectionate toward her. He wasn't having any trouble wrapping the tranquil Mahiru up in his arms.

"...I had better let Miss Koyuki know before too long, huh?"

It was only natural Mahiru wanted to tell the person who had been the most concerned with her well-being that she had finally found someone to love, that she was dating him, and that he treasured her this much.

"Let her know we've started dating?"

"Yes... And tell her I got my hands on my ideal partner."

"...Ideal? Me?"

"Of course, the main condition is that you love me, but...I've always thought I wanted someone who would respect me as a woman and treasure me, someone who would accept me for who I am."

In other words, Mahiru's ideal partner was a person who would respect her for who she was and love her. She was sure Amane fulfilled that ideal better than anyone else could.

She could say definitively that no other person would ever appear who would treasure her as much as he did, or understand her as well, or have such deep, attentive affection for her and her choices. To Mahiru, Amane was her star supporter, a ray of sunshine in her life.

"I'm honored that I meet your expectations, Mahiru."

"Actually, I was surprised I met your expectations. No matter how you look at it, I was the more tiresome of the two of us."

"You're putting yourself down too much."

"I mean..."

Though of course she knew, as everyone else did, that she was a capable person, only Mahiru herself knew how troubled she was on the inside.

A secretly bitter girl who wore the mask of an angel. A girl who got lonely and anxious easily. A girl who craved companionship from someone, anyone, and yet stubbornly refused to let anyone in. She was a bundle of contradictions. That was who Mahiru Shiina was.

Amane had made it past her stubborn defenses and taken the hand of the little girl who had been hiding on the other side.

He hadn't busted down the wall exactly, and he hadn't slipped through a crack, either; he had knocked boldly at the front door and faced her directly.

He had taken his time and waited for Mahiru to extend her hand to him.

Amane himself didn't seem to understand what a sincere and honest person he was. Men like him were truly hard to come by.

He really doesn't seem to be aware of it himself.

Depending on how they looked at him, some people might call Amane a loser, or judge him to be a pushover, but Mahiru thought those reflected Amane's most wonderful qualities.

That said, she couldn't deny in some ways he was too much of a late bloomer, and it was true she had felt impatient with him at times.

"I feel as if I'll never meet anybody more amazing than you, Mahiru."

"Oh no, are you settling for me?"

"No way, you know that's not what I mean… Actually, I don't have eyes for anyone else."

"…I know."

Even without him telling her, Mahiru knew perfectly well Amane only had eyes for her, and she couldn't keep herself from smiling.

But Amane pouted just a little. He must have thought she was laughing at him.

"Why are you smiling?"

"Oh, I guess I was just thinking again about what a lucky girl I am."

She doubted there was anyone who wouldn't be happy, feeling so much love from their beloved partner.

"...Mahiru, right now, are you happy?"

"Yes, I'm happy. Can't you tell by looking?"

When she wasn't playing the part of the angel or anything, when she was just ordinary Mahiru, she thought she was a very easy person to read. That was because she was just an ordinary girl, who responded to the things Amane did and said with ordinary human emotions.

When Mahiru looked up at Amane from within his arms, Amane's eyebrows drooped in relief, and his face softened into a smile when he saw her fully relaxed expression.

"...Mm, I'm glad," he whispered, and he sounded happy from the bottom of his heart.

It made Mahiru feel bashful. He was already holding her, but he hugged her tightly and drew her even closer to him. Amane's embrace was gentle yet powerful, as if to tell her she didn't have to go to the trouble of putting on an act for him.

"I'm going to try even harder than ever before, to make you even happier. If there are any ways I'm lacking or places where I'm inadequate, make sure you tell me so."

"Let me see. Sometimes you only think about me, and you let yourself be an afterthought. That's a really bad habit."

Amane's greatest shortcoming was that he had a tendency to neglect himself and say he was doing it for Mahiru's sake.

It didn't make her happy to be prioritized to the point that it harmed Amane, but Amane failed to notice that it didn't bring Mahiru any joy, because he was trying so hard.

If she didn't point out such things and chide him for them, it was liable to lead to problems for them down the line.

"I—I don't mean to do that, really... For me, it's like your happiness is my happiness, so if I can get you to smile, then I'm pleased, too."

"You're a real dummy, Amane."

"...How do you figure?"

"Because you must know by now that I'm the same way."

With how clever Amane was, he ought to understand what Mahiru was trying to say. Because they were both two of a kind.

Amane picked up on her meaning right away. He frowned, looking obviously dejected, and apologized. "...Sorry."

Mahiru smiled at him, feeling keenly how much she loved these honest parts of him. "It's really okay. I said this before, too, didn't I? I love you, Amane. When you're happy, I'm happy... So please, don't just prioritize me; make yourself a priority, too, okay?"

Just as Amane's happiness was tied to Mahiru's happiness, her happiness was tied to his.

Seeing the person she loved with a smile on his face, not suffering any hardships, delighted her more than anything else, and that alone was enough to make her feel deeply satisfied.

It was probably because they could both share those feelings that Mahiru felt so fortunate. She wanted to believe the same went for Amane.

"Please, let me make you happy as well, Amane. You want to find happiness *with* me, right?"

It was no good for Mahiru alone to be happy. It was no good for Mahiru to be happy without him.

The important thing was Amane *and* Mahiru were happy *together*.

Mahiru absolutely did not think she could be satisfied if either of them was wanting for happiness. That would eventually become the seeds of disaster.

"...Yeah."

©Hanekoto

Amane seemed a little bit tongue-tied. Mahiru watched to make sure his expression eventually melted into a sappy smile. Then, still situated between Amane's legs, Mahiru wriggled around to face him, sitting with her feet tucked underneath her.

Without pausing, she pressed her lips to Amane's, almost like she wanted to keep him from talking for a second. Peering into his face from point-blank range, she watched his expression shift from astonishment to a look of slight embarrassment and resignation as he pursed his lips tightly.

"...Are you happy now?"

When she smiled impishly at him, his eyes were very close to hers, and he gave her a soft look that was as good as voicing his surrender.

"...That might not be enough for me."

Amane also smiled impishly and, as if begging for more attention, put his arms around Mahiru's body and pulled her close as he buried his face in the base of her neck. It tickled her body and her heart, and Mahiru laughed quietly with a rebuke that was not quite a rebuke. "Geez," she said, and accepted his kisses.

In her diary entry for the day, which she hadn't finished yet, Mahiru decided she would write that, at the moment, she was very, very happy.

Afterword

Thank you very much for picking up a copy of this book.

My name is Saekisan, and I am your author. I trust you enjoyed the second volume of *Angel Next Door* short stories?

Getting right into it, Miss Koyuki, the Shiina family's housekeeper whose name had come up but who had not yet appeared in the main story, finally made her entrance. Actually, no matter how I tried, I couldn't find a good place for her in the main storyline, so if it wasn't in a format like this, I don't know if I ever would have arranged for her to make an appearance.

In her looks, Mahiru takes after her parents, but her overall personality is more like Miss Koyuki's; that's how her character's set up. Mahiru turned out the way she did because she was raised by Miss Koyuki, who was basically a super, all-powerful mother figure. Mahiru will probably also become somewhat like that in the future. Probably.

Besides that, since this was a bonus edition, I got to enjoy writing about Mahiru cuddling with Amane, sizing up Kadowaki, and already basically being married into the Fujimiya family.

Afterword

Itsuki and Chitose appeared a lot in the previous short-stories volume, so this time, I made Yuuta and Amane's parents the focus.

A couple of things I thought as I was writing this were: *"Amane is, like, incredibly dependable from Mahiru's point of view, huh...?"* and *"She sure is in love with him, huh...?"*

Well, it was already perfectly clear in the main storyline that she's head over heels for him, so I guess it was a little late for that!

Once again, Hanekoto drew wonderful illustrations for this volume.

The *Alice in Wonderland* parody illustrations Hanekoto drew for the special edition are something we'd probably never see in the main books, and I was writhing in agony over how cute they are. Mahiru really looks good in an apron dress… And I love Amane in bunny ears.

The cover for the regular edition is cute, too, you know… I felt like I'm not sure if we should be allowed to see Mahiru in her nightgown. She's a refined young lady, and yet somehow there's a glimmer of something alluring about her. Mahiru is really great.

The booklet included with the special edition has a gallery of illustrations by Hanekoto, which I'm really looking forward to seeing.

Even though I've got the digital version already, I still want my paper copy…!

Now we've reached the end, but I still need to thank everyone who helped me.

To the head editor who worked so hard to get this book published, to everyone in the editing department at GA Books, to everyone in the sales department, to the proofreaders, to Hanekoto, to everyone in the print shop, and to all of you who picked up a copy: truly, thank you so much.

Let's meet again in the next volume.

Thank you very much for reading to the end!

HAVE YOU BEEN TURNED ON TO LIGHT NOVELS YET?

86—EIGHTY-SIX, VOL. 1–13

In truth, there is no such thing as a bloodless war. Beyond the fortified walls protecting the eighty-five Republic Sectors lies the "nonexistent" Eighty-Sixth Sector. The young men and women of this forsaken land are branded the Eighty-Six and, stripped of their humanity, pilot "unmanned" weapons into battle...

Manga adaptation available now!

WOLF & PARCHMENT, VOL. 1–10

The young man Col dreams of one day joining the holy clergy and departs on a journey from the bathhouse, Spice and Wolf. Winfiel Kingdom's prince has invited him to help correct the sins of the Church. But as his travels begin, Col discovers in his luggage a young girl with a wolf's ears and tail named Myuri, who stowed away for the ride!

Manga adaptation available now!

SOLO LEVELING, VOL. 1–8

E-rank hunter Jinwoo Sung has no money, no talent, and no prospects to speak of—and apparently, no luck, either! When he enters a hidden double dungeon one fateful day, he's abandoned by his party and left to die at the hands of some of the most horrific monsters he's ever encountered.

Comic adaptation available now!

THE SAGA OF TANYA THE EVIL, VOL. 1-13

Reborn as a destitute orphaned girl with nothing to her name but memories of a previous life, Tanya will do whatever it takes to survive, even if it means living life behind the barrel of a gun!

Manga adaptation available now!

SO I'M A SPIDER, SO WHAT?, VOL. 1-16

I used to be a normal high school girl, but in the blink of an eye, I woke up in a place I've never seen before and—and I was reborn as a spider?!

Manga adaptation available now!

OVERLORD, VOL. 1-16

When Momonga logs in one last time just to be there when the servers go dark, something happens—and suddenly, fantasy is reality. A rogues' gallery of fanatically devoted NPCs is ready to obey his every order, but the world Momonga now inhabits is not the one he remembers.

Manga adaptation available now!

VISIT YENPRESS.COM TO CHECK OUT ALL OUR TITLES AND...

GET YOUR YEN ON!

Yen On | Yen Press